Cricklepit Combine_ _ _ _ _ _ _ _ 'problem cases': Tyke Ti_ _ _ _ _ _ _ _ _ _ _, jum-
per Cantello. But when Ferret was marched by his dad to
the front door on his first day there, feeling sick with
apprehension, he couldn't know that he too would
become one of its heroes.

His big problem was that he couldn't read — not that he
didn't want to, he just couldn't. And then there was the
bullying Magnus and his gang stealing kids' money,
while the teachers thought he could do no wrong.
Thank goodness, then, for Minty and Beany, and
Minty's mum . . . and Sir.

This fifth story about Cricklepit Combined, immortalized
in the award-winning *The Turbulent Term of Tyke Tiler*, is
another wonderfully witty Gene Kemp novel with all
the gritty realism of its predecessors.

Gene Kemp was born in the Midlands, the youngest of a
large family. A scholarship to a local Grammar School
was followed by an Exhibition to Exeter University
where she took a degree in English. She was awarded an
honorary degree from Exeter University in 1984. She
wrote her first children's book in 1972 and has since
written many more. Gene Kemp lives in Exeter. She has
three children and three grandchildren.

Gene Kemp

Just Ferret

ILLUSTRATED BY JON DAVIS

PUFFIN BOOKS

PUFFIN BOOKS

Published by the Penguin Group
Penguin Books Ltd, 27 Wrights Lane, London W8 5TZ, England
Viking Penguin, a division of Penguin Books USA Inc.
375 Hudson Street, New York, New York 10014, USA
Penguin Books Australia Ltd, Ringwood, Victoria, Australia
Penguin Books Canada Ltd, 2801 John Street, Markham, Ontario, Canada L3R 1B4
Penguin Books (NZ) Ltd, 182–190 Wairau Road, Auckland 10, New Zealand

Penguin Books Ltd, Registered Offices: Harmondsworth, Middlesex, England

First published by Faber and Faber Limited 1990
Published in Puffin Books 1991
10 9 8 7 6 5 4 3 2 1

For
Eleanor Edwards and Libby Sparkes

Characters in the book

At Cricklepit combined school –
Chief Sir – Headteacher
Mr Merchant – Deputy head
Mrs Flint – 4F's teacher
Mrs Ferndale – Supply teacher
Mrs Malpas – Helper and minder

Chief characters in 4F   *Parents*
Magnus   Mark's mother (Mrs Saunders)
Striker ⎫   Minty's Mum
Sean   ⎬ his Meanies   Joe Hardacre (Ferret's Dad)
Ceefax ⎭   Mr Reynolds (Magnus's Dad)
Mark (Beany)
Penelope   *Others*
Minty   Old Man
Kelly   The Joker
Duncan   Three Cats
Peter   The Girl
Gary

and of course: Owen Hardacre (the Ferret)

Ferret's story was taped and recorded by William
Merchant as part of his Reading Research Project.

I hide my work.
Sometimes I wish
I could hide myself
away forever.

'I hide my work.
Sometimes I wish
I could hide myself
away forever.'

Darrell Bond, aged 10.

Supplied by the British Dyslexia Association

Chapter One

'You don't know me . . . but that ain't no matter.'
Huckleberry Finn: Mark Twain

SID: *I'm going to keep this gorilla under my bed.*
BILL: *But what about the smell?*
SID: *He'll just have to get used to it.*

It took Dad just over a week before he got round to registering me at the new school. Every time I could see the blurry outlines of the idea forming like a bubble over his head, I disappeared or got busy or fetched him something else to think about, like a can of beer. So time slithered away while I sussed out yet another new neighbourhood, wondering if I'd be able to settle here, and tried to forgive him for dragging me on again, this time to this cissy-soft place, where they all speak as if they've got plums in their mouths or burr away like something out of the sticks.

I'll not bore you wi' the getting here. Either you've ridden in a hundred-year-old van held together wi' spit and string, all your gear piled on the roof or in the back so you can't see out, or you haven't, so you either know or you don't. Plus the Joker, our dog, playing merry hell. The Joker doesn't care for his routine being disturbed none, unless he disturbs it

1

himself – like taking himself off for a week at a time: that's OK by him, but driving miles across country – no. That's not for the Joker. I've not seen him for three days now but he'll turn up when he's hungry. In this household we don't fret much if someone don't turn up once in a while 'cos, as Dad says, life gets pretty unbearable unless you can get away from it.

But there came a day, Monday it was, and Dad recovering from a heavy Sunday session, so he was spaced out all morning, but coming through it at lunchtime, his temper vile, and me just about to take to the woods for the day, when he said:

'Make some strong coffee. Get on with it. Don't hang about. What's the matter with you? Paralysed?'

Full of Olde Worlde Charm, Dad.

I made coffee and cut sarnies while he indicated with much mitt waving that I sit down and listen to His Words of Wisdom. This occurs from time to time. It was one of these sessions that got us here in the first place.

'This has gone on long er.ɔugh. Money's running out. Tomorrow I start work.'

'Oh, yeah.'

'Oh, yeah. And less o' that from you. There's bin enough laying about. This afternoon – *school*.'

I got up to leave but he pushed me down. He's old an' unfit but he's still stronger than half a dozen blokes so I didn't argue.

'Lionel says Cricklepit Combined's the one.'

Lionel's the bloke we're shacking up with until we get a place of our own (joke). He's the biggest phoney on the face of the earth.

'But I was at a Comp. last place . . .'

'When you bothered to turn up . . .'

'Don't go on, Dad. Why not the Comp. here?'

'The ages are different. Don't ask me why. Cricklepit takes twelves, so this year Cricklepit Combined, next year, the Comp.'

'If we're still here.'

'This time I'm settling down. And shut up, won't you. Always on the yap. It's a good school. Lionel went there years ago.'

'That's no recommendation!'

'Shut up, I say. Give it a chance. We're starting fresh here. No more mitching. You ain't learnt nuthing with all them years o' schooling. Let's see what this place can do. And do some work. You can't even read yet!'

'Can't see reading's done much for you. You've got all the way – where? Fifty useless paintings nobody'll buy and lodging with Lionel – in this dump.'

'Only temporary, son. Till I get sorted out.'

'What then? Think you can afford a place round

here? It's yuppie territory. With a few millionaires thrown in.'

'Not all of it, not all. Anyway, *they'll* buy a few pictures, won't they?'

'Not your old rubbish, they won't . . .'

But I'd gone too far. There are only a few things my dad cares about, Joker the dog, beer and his paintings – you don't put the mockers on them.

'ENOUGH!' he roared. 'Git yourself cleaned up. And get a move on.'

'It's not easy here in this dump.'

'Oh, git on with it. You can't be a complete moron, though come to think of it you could well be. Twelve years old and can't read. How come I ever got you? You don't even look like me!'

'Since you're six foot two with a ginger beard, I'm glad I don't. I often wish you weren't my Dad, anyway.'

He got up to bash me but the Joker rushed in, all ribs, ears and tail wagging. In the uproar Dad cooled down.

But not far enough to save me . . .

He flannelled me himself, yuck, and hauled me off to buy new trainers and awful grey trousers. Still some money left, I noticed. And an unspeakable grey shirt and even a tie, though by the time we'd finished tying it between us it looked grotty enough to be put-up-able with. We didn't get to school that day.

However, Dad was keen that the next would definitely see me there. But morning got lost discussing The Meaning of Art with Lionel (double yuck) and it was afternoon before we set off by the river and up towards this school, me dragging as much as possible, naturally.

It was hot. The river flowed along. I could've stayed by it for ever. The only thing I'd seen to like so far.

'Get a move on,' Dad said.

Later,

'I said get a move on,' he encouraged me with a blow on the back which sent me to my knees.

'You are a wimp,' he said.

'Don't talk like that at the school, Dad. And no swear words, please. Sometimes you're more swear than words.'

'Artists' licence, son. Besides, I know how to behave. Your grandmother brought me up very strictly. Better brought up than you . . .'

'Whose fault's that?'

'Your mother's. She should never have run off.'

'She'd have to have been a saint to stand living with you.'

'She warn't no saint. You've got her nasty, pasty looks.'

'Shurrup, will ya?'

I ran on – then remembered where I was heading for. I turned back. A last try.

'Dad, I don't think it's right to turn up at a school at three o'clock in the afternoon.'

'We'll sign you on. You can start properly tomorrow.'

Into my mind came all the hassle. Again.

'What book were you on at your last school?'

'See if you can read this.'

'Can you write a story for me?'

'No? Well – see if you can copy this. Do your best.'

Do your best! I couldn't do any of that.

I *could* cook a roast, pluck a chicken, skin a rabbit,

5

mend a fuse, sew, bake a cake – I could drive a tractor and a car but you keep quiet about things like that. I could shoot too, make a workable bow and arrow, pick out a tune on the piano, or play the recorder or flute. I could strum on a guitar, play an accordion and a mouth organ (a bit), climb a cliff, swim a mile – in a river at that – open a Yale lock with a plastic card, I could play draughts or chess, I could add up as fast as a calculator, do any Maths as long as it was figures – my mum ran off when I was six, you see, leaving me with *him*, and *he* does nothing much except paint and drink – so with him I had to learn to survive.

BUT I CAN'T READ – SO
I CAN'T WRITE.

And I don't want to go to another new school. I didn't want to go to *any* school. I'm sick of 'em and not being able to read. I didn't want to be here. There's nothing I want here, nothing for me.

A red-brick building, old, with a bell-tower, smaller than my last Comp. and ordinary, with an asphalt playground, railings and a small playing field. The only thing different – in the middle of the play-ground, a huge green tree. The branches only started half-way up, I noticed. Dad marched to the front door.

I felt sick.

Chapter Two

I like the idea of putting jokes on each chapter. Some of them were pretty funny. Here are some of my jokes.

'Why couldn't the hedgehog wash his hair?'
'Because he left his head and shoulders on the motorway.'
Sent by Sam Little, Heathfield School (Taunton)

Dead quiet. As quiet as midnight when everybody's asleep . . . only it wasn't midnight and we weren't asleep, this old guy the Headmaster and me outside this classroom which was silent as the grave. All the others we'd walked past had been classroom-noisy, you know, but this one, not a sound, not a peep. Was anybody in there? Or had they all died? Or vanished for ever like the crew on that ship, the *Marie Celeste* my dad told me about, sailing for ever with nobody on board? Or perhaps they had some sort of torture chamber in there – no, you'd hear screams. But maybe this old Headteacher lured kids to their doom . . . do 'em in . . . trust Dad to push off as soon as he'd dumped me here and filled in a form.

Then he turned and smiled. I wanted to say:

'Can I just go away now, please. I've been to school. Will that do?'

I could see the old building had been knocked about a bit, the doorway opened up, then a red plastic sliding door fixed across. It had 4F written on it. He pulled at this sliding door, which didn't budge though it buckled a bit.

'Ah – Mr Merchant's taking 4F this afternoon. He'll be reading a story and he doesn't welcome interruptions. And rightly so. But you're an exception, aren't you, boy?'

He beamed at me and pushed at the door again. Was he some sort of nut, I wondered? It was so easy to open that door. I'd do it for him but it wasn't me who wanted to go in the classroom and if we hung about long enough the afternoon would be over (I hoped).

A minute later I couldn't stand seeing him fumbling with the door any longer so I slid it across, then followed him through.

Into the silence and into the eyes. All of them staring at me. No one smiling. Just those eyes looking – looking at me – the alien, the enemy, the wild animal. They looked as if they'd been waiting for something to happen . . . and bad luck, that something happened to be me.

Someone sighed. Someone shuffled their feet. Some of the eyes looked away. A tall swotty-looking girl stood up.

The Headteacher spoke:

'I'm sorry to interrupt, Mr Merchant and everybody . . . no, sit down, Penelope, gratifying though it is to have one of the class stand, the rest being paralysed, presumably . . .'

'Good afternoon, Sir,' they chorused, lurching to their feet. A funny looking one, skinnier than anybody had any right to be, sort of half stood, then

9

collapsed down on ten-foot stick legs. This 4F lot looked as miserable as if I'd snatched a box of chocolates off them.

'I expect you wanted to hear the end of Mr Merchant's story,' the Headteacher burbled. 'Sorry about that but I want you to meet Owen, Owen Hardacre. He'll be in your class. Make him welcome. Goodbye Owen, Mr Merchant, 4F.'

He had a word with Mr Merchant, then hummed himself out of the classroom. This Mr Merchant grinned at me, wrote something down and as he did so the voices started, very low – but my hearing's super good.

'Owen Hardacre . . .' nudge, nudge, giggle.

'It's a spook.'

'An albino.'

'ET.'

'A goblin.'

A boy built like a sumo wrestler scratched monkey-fashion.

'No, it's a ferret. A ferret, I say. Look, white hair, pink eyes.'

The one who said the ferret bit was big and handsome, black hair, blue eyes, piranha teeth. Dad says I ain't learnt nuthin' at all those schools I've been to. Maybe. Maybe not books. I learned to read one thing though, and that boy was trouble. Bad trouble. I guessed the others round him would be his gang, his yes-men. And I could see this nicely-dressed-in-uniform-listening-so-quietly class had a sharp edge to it. This would not be easy. I wished I wasn't there.

'Ferrets. Ferrets in trousers,' giggled an ant-eater boy, all conk.

Then someone spoke out loud.

10

'Please go on with the story, Sir. It was beautiful. Sort of shivery.'

The girl who said this smiled at Sir, then at me. She had a lovely smile, the best thing I'd seen (along with the river) since I'd landed here with Dad.

And swotty-girl Penelope said, 'Yes, do go on reading, Mr Merchant.'

But he closed his book.

'No, we'll save it for next time. Ceefax – I mean Colin – if you want to live to the end of the afternoon, stop giggling like a demented hyena . . . Right, clear up everyone. Ready for Mrs Flint.'

'I'm here already,' said a voice from the doorway.

The teacher who stood there holding a pile of books was young and pretty (for a teacher) with golden hair piled on her head and very blue eyes and a peachy-clean complexion, wearing a smart suit. Walking past the teachers' cars, I'd spotted a car so shiny and new it made the rest look like wrecks. That'd be hers, I thought now. She was just the same. She took no notice of Mr Merchant easing his way out, stopping to have a word with the beanpole and saying 'See you tomorrow, Owen,' to me, but told everyone to clear their things nicely and go home quietly. Her words were smoothed and sanded down but underneath . . .?

'You're new, aren't you?' she said to me. 'You should have been brought to me first. What's your name?'

I told her and waited for:

What were you reading at your last school? But she didn't say that.

'I'll have a word with the Headteacher, then talk to

11

you tomorrow. You can go, now. Oh, we all try to wear uniform here. Your trousers are fine but you'll need different shoes, a blazer and a new tie. Let your mother know.'

'I haven't got a mother.'

'Oh, dear.' She sighed crossly as if I'd deliberately lost her somewhere. 'You do have a father?'

'Yes.'

'I'll be in touch.' That should be funny, him and her, I thought. 'Off you go, now. Oh, by the way, a big, ugly dog has been left, tied by a piece of string, to a gate forbidden to the children as there are other safer ones to use. Could it be yours?'

'Dad must have left the Joker behind to see me home.'

'That won't be necessary in future. Goodbye, Owen. Be here at eight-forty sharp tomorrow morning. *We* like an early start.'

Her voice held all the warmth of the inside of a fridge-freezer.

She hurried away. I'd been dealt with.

'Owen,' someone said and the beanpole limped towards me on stick insect legs. He looked terrible. There could be worse things than not being able to read, I reckoned. What did he want? Waiting for him to get to me was painful for both of us so I moved towards him. But a woman got there first.

'Beany,' she said, sort of pleading.

He looked choked.

'*Parents* are supposed to *wait* at the gate. *Parents* don't collect fourth years from classrooms. I'm not a baby,' he scowled.

Too true. Stood up straight he'd be nearly six foot

12

tall. Taller than high, wide and handsome, Piranha Face. Come to think of it, where had he got to? I didn't want him on my back. Ever.

Beany and his mum started to argue, so I headed for the front door. I didn't much want to hang around here.

And just outside in the playground was high, wide and handsome, Piranha Face, waiting together with the Sumo Wrestler, the Ant-eater and a boy who looked as if he was brain-dead. I wasn't sure they meant trouble for me but I didn't especially want to find out just then. I'd rather not know. I doubled back to find another door to to leave by. This is not easy when you're on strange territory and haven't a clue where anywhere is, and it came as no surprise to find them all waiting outside the next one I arrived at (when I found it). Maybe it was just coincidence, but I don't need this pressure on, I sang to myself, back-pedalling speedily into the rabbit warren of a school. This time I ran into Beany and his mum. He looked panda-eyed and worried, and as if he was trying to tell me something, warn me maybe?

But I don't need any warning, I wanted to say. I've met Piranha Face and his like before – they're always around wherever you go. But not someone like you, Beany – you're new to me, different.

'Beany wonders if you'd like a lift?' his mother asked. A nice lady, that one.

'No.'

She looked surprised. I don't think people said no to her much. She looked as if her life had been pretty cushy – except . . . she'd got Beany. What was wrong with him?

'Oh. You're sure? We'll go then, Beany.'

He followed her out slowly, still half-turning to me. It seemed like a good idea to walk out close behind them. She stopped to have a word with Piranha Face and his lads and I saw them turn into different people, all toothy beams and, 'Yes, Mrs Saunders' and 'No, Mrs Saunders'. She smiled back. Beany didn't. Somehow, I thought, he wanted to see me out of the gate. He couldn't know I'd got the Joker tied up at the wrong gate. And how could he know that they didn't scare me, since the only things that do that are *reading* and Dad in his black moods! And yet, I didn't feel I wanted to tangle with Piranha Face if I could help it.

Stop hanging about, kid. Freedom's out there. For tonight, anyway, the sun's shining, the Joker's waiting patiently, nose on paws, ignoring the world. I run towards him and he stretches up, enough to scare anyone, a great grey wolf of a dog with one floppy yellow ear, and he near knocks me flat as he stands upright, paws on shoulders, greeting me. Good ole Joker. I untie him. Come on now, fast. I'll race you. Run, run. Down to the river. Tonight we'll explore. Come on, come on, come on, Joker. Like the wind, the wind. Down to the river!

Chapter Three

Distracted the Mother Said to her Boy

Distracted the mother said to her boy
'Do you try to upset and perplex and annoy?
Now, give me four reasons – and don't play the fool –
Why you shouldn't get up and get ready for school.'

Her son replied slowly, 'Well, mother, you see,
I can't stand the teachers and they detest me;
And there isn't a boy or girl in the place
That I like or, in turn, that delights in my face.'

'And I'll give you two reasons,' she said, 'Why you ought
Get yourself off to school before you get caught;
Because, first, you are forty and, next, you young fool,
It's your job to be there.
You're the head of the school.'

Gregory Harrison

Next day when I got to school without the Joker, the kids were gathering under the tree in the playground. In ones and twos they came, then threes and fours, then more and more. The Boss, Piranha Face from 4F, himself, stood up on a bench under the tree, flanked by his mates. I looked around – nobody else had his power, his clout, though the tall one that the

Headteacher had called Penelope was there with a crowd of girls round her. I hung around on the outskirts, hoping to pick up ends of conversation – that's what you do when you're new. I looked for Beany. I couldn't see him. But there was the girl who smiled. She saw me and stretched out a hand to pull me through near to the tree with her.

'What's going on?' I whispered.

'Chief Sir's leaving. That's the Headmaster. We've just heard.'

I tuned into the voices. The jungle tom-toms were sending out the news, all right.

'He can't be. He's always bin here, someone said.'

'He is. He is. I tell you.'

'He's taking early retirement. *He* told my mother. *I've* known about it for ages.'

'That's Penelope,' whispered the girl. 'She's the school genius.'

'What's your name?'

'Minty. What's yours? Oh, it's Owen, isn't it?'

'They'll call me Ferret.'

'Don't you mind?'

'No, it's happened before. I couldn't care less.'

'It can't be *early* retirement. 'e must be an 'undred, at least.'

'It's not early enough. Should've been got rid of ages ago.'

'Stands to reason.'

''e was 'ere when they started the school.'

'Don't be stupid. It was founded in 1665,' shouted Penelope.

'So?'

'He'd be over three hundred years old.'

'So? Wrinklies are about that age.'

'My mother told me not to tell you all but he won't mind now. He's been waiting to retire for ages,' said Penelope.

'Why are you crying?' I asked Minty.

'I like him. I don't want him to go. We had Miss Plum, she was lovely, then she left and Mrs Flint came and it all changed. That's what happens.'

'What's the big boy called?'

'Magnus. Any minute now he'll tell us all what to do. That's his gang there, Striker, you've seen him, then Sean, he's horrible, they're all horrible, and Ceefax.'

'Ceefax?'

'The one with the big nose. He thinks he knows everything, like Penelope. But he gets everything wrong. So we call him Ceefax.'

She'd stopped crying.

'In this school', she said, 'Magnus rules the boys,

Penelope the girls.' She started to giggle, 'I say it's sexist. But it may not be 'cos Magnus and Penelope *both* want to rule the world.'

'Shut up, everyone!' yelled Striker, the hefty one. 'Magnus wants a word.'

'Magnus!!' Magnus stretched up, flexing his muscles.

'A good send-off for Chief Sir! That's what we need! The teachers will ask you to give money for a present. We'll give them some, but bring half to me, Penelope or Striker. Got that clear. For our own *private* surprise. For Chief Sir.'

'Yeah! Great! Brill!' shouted the kids. 'Good ole Magnus. Three cheers . . .'

He held up his hand.

'Hold it. We don't want the teachers here. It's time to go in. *Remember*, kids. This is *our* surprise. You know what to do!'

They started to move away. I couldn't believe it. Amazing. Was it always like this, at this school? I didn't know what to say to the girl. I didn't know who I could trust here. If anyone. Maybe it was just my suspicious mind.

'Minty . . .' I began, 'tell me . . .'

Someone jostled us. I looked round. Striker had joined us.

'Why, it's our little Ferret . . . Minty, you always did pick funny friends.'

I walked as fast as I could to the classroom. No hassle there, I hoped. Except for the Reading. We'd have to get to grips with that, sooner or later.

'You've done all this Maths very well,' said Mrs Flint. 'Quite a surprise. Accurate and fairly neat. But why didn't you do this section? Didn't you have time? I gave you plenty.'

I was a small sliced-off bit of louse in a slide under a microscope and Mrs Flint was examining me with her sparkly blue eye. The small sliced-off bit of louse said nothing. It wouldn't, would it?

'Now, come on. Why did you leave out these? They're no more difficult than the others. Easier, in fact.'

Silence everywhere. I'd never known such a quiet class as this one. I almost missed that old Comprehensive I used to go to. At least it had been noisy. Minty looked up and gave me a quick smile that vanished almost before it began. Beany, who'd arrived late and not been told off, I noticed, looked at me with his sad eyes like a giant panda.

'Come along, Owen. You're not the only one in this class who needs attention. Tell me about these you left out.'

OK, out with it. I might as well come out with it.

'They're written problems. And I can't read. So I couldn't do them, could I?'

'You can't read? How old are you? Twelve? You can't read *at all*?' Tough undernotes were thundering up under the silky top voice.

Piranha Face sat up smartish, all eyes and ears (as well as the teeth).

'No.'

'Well, what have you been messing about for for all those years?'

'Dunno.'

'You must know. Come on. You speak well enough. I don't think you're *very* stupid though I can see you've no support at home. With regard to *that*, do make an effort to keep tidy yourself as you're not a baby now. But this reading . . .'

A crash. A book fell. Beany had hauled himself to his legs, and it hurt as you could see from his face. Slowly he made his way to Mrs Flint's desk. She'd stopped looking at me, gee t'anks.

'Please excuse me, Mrs Flint . . .'

'Mark, I'm busy with Owen.'

'It's about Owen. I expect he's dyslexic. That's why he can't read. My cousin was and he was very clever, really. He got all his exams. C-c-can I help Owen? I'll hear him read, Mrs Flint. Please.'

Did her face soften a little? Just a little bit. Keep fingers crossed. Beany hearing me read I could stand. I wouldn't go out of my head like I had once at that other school. She thought about it.

'No, it wouldn't do. You miss so much being away, Mark, you can't afford to waste more time. You've all those Science notes to copy out. Besides, he'll have to have tests and expert treatment. In the meantime while we carry on with our folders, Penelope shall hear him temporarily. She can best afford the time. And Mark, you should've been attending to your own work, not listening to us. Penelope?'

'Yes, Mrs Flint.'

Penelope leapt up, eager-beaver. She'd been listening too. In fact all the class had their ears pinned forward.

'Just give me some resources, Mrs Flint, and we'll dive in. Eh, Owen? We'll soon get you going, won't we?'

Watching Beany drag his way back to his seat, I couldn't believe it. Fate, why had you got it in for me today?

'He can't read. Can't read at all,' was hissed from the back of the class.

'By the way, Mark,' Mrs Flint said. 'Not being able to read doesn't always mean dyslexia. And people aren't quite sure what they mean by it. Probably not in this case.'

I wanted to wipe that sniff straight off her face. She concentrated on me again.

'Owen, you told me you hadn't a mother. Or any woman . . . living with you.'

'No.'

'You live with your father?'

'Mm.'

'What does he do?'

'A painter.'

'Oh, he paints and decorates, does he?'

'Not very often. He hates painting and decorating.'

'But you said . . .'

'He paints pictures. Real pictures. Oils and acrylics and water colours. Sometimes he does woodcuts.'

She looked at me as if she couldn't take it in.

'Oh. Well, Penelope – here, use this book with Owen. In that corner there. Do what you can.'

Then she frowned the class into silence.

The book was a Janet and John Book Three – as old as the hills from the look of it. I knew the cover well. But not the words. In the half-hour that followed Penelope did all the speaking. I refused to say anything at all. I wouldn't look at the book, either.

Chapter Four

'Why did the hedgehog cross the road?'
To see his flat mate.'

Sam Little, once more

VISIT THE QUAY!
FUN TIME FOR THE FAMILY

THE
MARITIME MUSEUM

Boats From All Over The World
See
THE CUSTOMS HOUSE
THE GREAT WAREHOUSES
as featured on television

HAVE A DAY OUT!

Hire a canoe, ride on the ferry, visit the craft
workshops, the potteries, the leisure centre.
Don't miss the antique market!
Cafés, restaurants, wine bars,
ancient inns full of nostalgia.

IT'S ANOTHER WORLD

Tourist Board

This is the place we've come to. Is this where my dad hopes to sell his pictures? His aren't *much* like the ones I've seen on the quay. No one could call *his* pictures pretty.

Rising up behind this world, shutting it into a basin, a red cliff drops down, whoosh, tall trees and grand old houses on the top, warehouses, shops, the rest built into the bottom. Not much further along are very ungrand houses, nearly ready to topple down the hill, the bottom one held up by a large beam – that's Lionel's. Just being in it makes you feel seasick, one side of a room a foot lower than the other and it's on the slide to the river. When I go to sleep on my little ole camp bed, I wonder if I'll wake up to find me in the water.

Further along on the other side you'll find the Night Life of the City, the nightclubs and so on. You should hear it at turning-out time. BOOM! BOOM! BANG! BANG! CRASH! SPLAT! That's how it is.

Near us is an amusement arcade with all the usual in there, fruit machines and the rest, what have you. A hundred ways to lose your money, while lights flash and music plays and the beat goes boom-boom-boompetty-boom. I don't go there much. You need money.

When I got in that afternoon Lionel was fast asleep, snoring like a rhinoceros, and Dad was painting like a demon in the room upstairs he'd grabbed for a studio. He looked up for two seconds and shouted above some opera or other going full blast.

'Meat and veg. downstairs. Make one of your casseroles. Gotta repay ole Lionel for his hospitality. When you've done that exercise Hound Dog for me.

Good kid. Oh, and change the tape. Don't want to stop. It's going well.'

He wouldn't have done the cooking anyway. But I wasn't bothered. What Dad tells you to do, you do. Mind you, I yelled, 'Want arsenic in it for flavour?'

He didn't hear. Paintbrush was going as fast as the Joker's tail. He was raring to go – so when I made the casserole and shoved it in the oven, we set out for the crowded quay where it was still hot with lots of people about. Just for a laugh, I shoved my last 10p into a machine in the amusement arcade, and who should I spot but Magnus and his Merry Men at a machine on the far side. They hadn't noticed me and as the 10p brought me no luck at all, I 'opped it, thinking no company's better than theirs. Don't think they saw me, being totally gone as the machine clattered winnings and they cheered.

I went in the other direction – past the stylish furniture place, shops, offices, the lot and then at last, turned into a narrow, murky opening hidden by an enormous bush covered with purple flowers and swarming with bees and wasps, keeping people out, but not me.

And there was the dark green shining leat (that's what Dad said it was called), where the ducks swim but not the swans, it not being posh enough for them, a secret world of high red walls and a path by the water, overgrown with trees and bushes and ferns and climbers, with moss and daisies – I know *their* names – springing out of the broken bricks of the wall dropping down to the green bottom of the leat. Trees and leaves hide everything, so that you can only just see that on the other bank are derelict buildings, shattered windows, rotten planks of wood with bits of corrugated iron where the roofs have fallen in. It's gloomy, rotten, falling down, broken down and yesterday a dead rat lay on the path. Anything could happen here in this secret place.

And it's beautiful. Green, mossy, cool and mysterious. Sunlight shines, making the leaves camouflage shadows. No new Cricklepit suspension bridge here, just a rusty iron girder crossing over the leat to an ancient wooden water wheel, flaking and rotten and old, old, old. I could look at it for ages. I might – I just might draw it some time. Tomorrow maybe? There again, I might not. One artist in a family's enough.

The Joker lay panting – he'd chased a squirrel and lost the race – so I shared a packet of crisps with him and the bacon sarnies I'd made to tide us over till Dad decided it was stew-eating time.

It was quiet, and as I sat there bits of First Day At A New School floated through my head.

Beany – real name Mark Saunders – had his own diet ready for him when we queued for lunch. He didn't want it, he said. I wouldn't have wanted it either.

'Stay with *him*. You'll be OK then,' said that Minty (did *she* have a real name?), grabbing me at the end of the morning.

'Whatjer mean?' I asked. 'What is this?'

'D'you like pizza? I think we've got some today. Mind you, you'll have to eat lettuce with it. New health food.'

'I can't follow you. What you on about?'

'You don't have to follow *me*. I'm no use to anyone. It's Beany you stay with. Hello, Penelope. Did you win that latest competition you went in for?'

25

'Yes, I did, actually. It'll be announced in the paper next week.'

'How wonderful! Penelope's the cleverest girl in the school, Owen. She's a genius.'

'Oh, I wouldn't say that, Minty. People can do anything they want if they try,' said Penelope, full of modesty. We'd already met.

I kept quiet as she gave me a very peculiar stare. With any luck she'd think I couldn't talk as well as not being able to read, so I did my spastic bit. We walked along very slowly, Beany, Minty, Penelope and me. What a funny place, I thought, what am I doing here? They're all bloomin' mad. Then Beany managed to grin at me, though his face was sheet white – well, not our sheets, they don't get changed often – but he looked awful. I got ready to catch him if he fell – but that grin was so cheeky, as if he knew what I was thinking. I thought once again that not being able to read wasn't bad compared with whatever was happening to him.

Later, to Minty.

'What did you mean, stay by him? And then talking about pizzas?'

She looked round, then said,

'Remember two things. One, it's pretty safe when you're with Beany as no one dares to touch him. Two, watch what you say here. It might get to the wrong ears.'

'You're crazy.'

'Yeah. Everyone says that. Come on, what you gonna do now? There's a squash club, a stamp club, a badminton club, a book club – oh, you wouldn't want that . . .'

26

'Well, you'd say, go with Beany, wouldn't you?'

'Uh-huh. That'll be the Stamp Club. He'll be back in a minute from his medication.'

'What's wrong with him?'

'He's ill.'

'I can see that. But what's wrong?'

'Well, your guess is as good as the doctor's, from what I hear.'

'Oh. Are you coming to the Stamp Club?'

'No way. Bores me silly. I'm off to the Art Room. Here's Beany now. See ya.'

The afternoon was quiet enough. I filled in exercise books etc. But all the time I knew I was being watched.

'Moron,' said the one they called Ceefax as he brushed past me in class.

Time to get back. To Dad and the casserole.

'Come on, boy,' I said and we set off back to Lionel's place. Out of curiosity I poked my head round the door of amusement arcade. Magnus and his mates were still in there.

'Must have loadsamoney,' I thought, and was just going to slip away, for thoughts of that casserole swam through my head, when . . .

'There's that dog,' one of them cried. 'You know. The dog that was tied up at school.'

'Ferret's dog. Old Moron,' said another – and this one was Magnus.

'Let's git 'im.'

It was time for me and the dog to leave at speed. The Joker can run twice as fast as I can, and I let him have plenty of rope, so that he'd tow me along. All the same, they were catching me up 'cos their legs were longer than mine. Striker was yelling about what he liked doing to spooks, ferrets and aliens, and it wasn't nice. I just kept running. It was not the time for witty answers. I didn't want any part of this. It had been a long day, the first at this school, I'd tried hard and now I was knackered, wanting my supper.

An unhappy idea came into my head. We were near the water.

'Chuck 'im in the river,' shouted one of them. They'd thought of it, too. I didn't think they'd dare but I didn't want to find out.

Magnus had gone ahead, the other three fanning out to surround me, so I stopped dead and hauled the Joker to me, kneeling down beside him.

'Kill, Joker, kill,' I growled in my throat.

They paused, circling round, unsure. The Joker growled in his throat, too. A menacing sound, I

hoped. They looked uncertain.

'He'll tear you apart,' I shouted.

They'd got me to the edge of the river, a bollard to the right and left and the four all facing me.

'Go for them, Joker,' I shouted and prayed.

And my prayers were answered. Arm in arm with his wife, hat on head, appeared Chief Sir. He lifted his hat in the air.

'Good evening, boys!'

His wife smiled at us all. We all smiled back, nice boys playing on a warm June evening.

'Good evening, Sir,' we chorused.

'Lovely night for a walk by the river,' she murmured.

And on Chief Sir and his wife went together. Everyone melted away. As for me, I skedaddled like the wind, saying thank you over and over again, for although he looks like a great grey and yellow wolf, you see, the Joker's a rotten fighter, a born coward. When he's really up against trouble he runs away or rolls over on his back and waves his paws in the air. That's the reason my dad calls him the Joker.

Chapter Five

'What question can never be answered by yes?'
'Are you asleep?'

If I'd known the kind of day it was gonna be I'd've gone back to bed and stayed there.

It was hard enough getting up as it was. Lionel's friends had joined us and they stayed the night. In the morning I picked my way among the bodies as I got some cornflakes, let out the Joker and shambled off to school. One of them who usually slept in the camp bed I was in, decided that's where he'd crash out. I got rid of him with a good kick but not before the bed collapsed and I had to put it together again. A rotten night.

I was late. Of course.

'I shall have to make a note of the time of your arrival,' Mrs Flint said. 'We like to maintain certain standards here. No, don't make excuses. You're late and you look slovenly. I shan't ask if you washed. Just go to the cloakroom and tidy yourself. Use plenty of soap and paper towels.'

'Those paper towels'll wipe half me face off.'

Her eyes glittered.

'We don't appreciate that type of humour here. And be grateful that you have free use of them.'

Doesn't anyone ever laugh? What a miserable place. Yet old Lionel was rabbiting on last night about the wonderful times he had. Wonderful times? Huh! Then I heard a roar of laughter through the classroom door I was walking past – Mr Merchant's. I might've guessed. Beany told me about the things they used to do in that class but for me it was fun yesterday, fun tomorrow, misery today.

When I got back to the classroom they were working on graphs and shapes, which was OK. Madame Flint said so, as if it hurt.

'Surprisingly neat and well thought out. Achieve that standard in your other work and your personal appearance and we might begin to get somewhere.'

'She's trying hard with you. You're doing all right,' whispered Minty, on her way past.

'What's she like if she *really* hates you, then?'

'Minty, don't waste time. Shakespeare made Richard II say, "I wasted time and now doth time waste me." Don't let it happen to you.'

A laugh a minute here.

But this wasn't bad except for waiting for Happy Reading Hour to arrive. And, like Christmas, it came at last. But it wasn't merry.

Kids moved into groups, each group on a different book. They had to answer questions about it, when they'd finished.

'Miss . . .'

'Call me Mrs Flint, please, Minty.'

'This is a lovely book, *Tom's Midnight Garden*. I can see it in my mind like a dream, like the dreams Tom has. Answering questions spoils the dream.'

'Oh, no. The questions will *help* your imagination.'

31

I stood by *her* desk, Odd Kid Out, as ever, wishing I was somewhere else.

'Yes, Owen. I have some spelling lists for you to practise.'

'I can't wait,' I muttered.

'What did you say?'

'Nothing, Miss.'

'My name is Mrs Flint.'

'Yes, Miss – Missus Flint. I thought I was having some tests.'

Even tests seemed better than spelling lists.

'This afternoon, you will see Mr Merchant and the Headmaster and they will test you.'

'Oh, goody.'

'What did you say?'

'Hadn't I better wait for the tests before I do the spellings?'

'No. Every little helps. Penelope, dear . . .'

'Yes, Mrs Flint?'

'Will you go through these with Owen?'

'Yes, of course, Mrs Flint. But he wouldn't speak to me yesterday.'

'In that case – Magnus – come here, you're in the same group . . .'

'Let me help Owen,' Beany called out. 'I've finished my book.'

'I know you have – dear' (this 'dear' sounded ever so false on her), 'but I do want you to catch up on missed notes so I'll use Magnus. Take Owen into the book corner and practise these sounds.'

He came over, piranha teeth on full splitting grin.

'Yes, I'll help him.'

'Not him,' I said. 'Mrs Flint, somebody else. Please.'

'Magnus is a very clever, sensible boy. He sets a good example. Off you go, Owen.'

Magnus's face had a leer on it that could have polluted the North Sea even further. He grabbed my arm, pinched it hard and hauled me along to the book corner. There, we sat together over the horrible lists.

'Come along, moron,' he said softly. 'C-A-T, cat. Say that after me, Owen, dear.'

I kicked his shin under the table.

'Ouch! I'll get you for that later. Now, spastic. B-A-T-, bat, M-A-T, mat, F-A-T, fat. I'll torture you tonight very slowly on the quay, before I push you into the river. People drown there, you know.'

I brought my elbow down hard on the fingers holding the lists.

That fetched 'im. He brought his foot down on my instep under the table and his face close to mine. It sent me nearly bananas with pain and his big eyes and big nose and big mouth wobbled in front of me, especially the mouth, as he whispered,

'You undersized, miserable ferret, we don't want you. I've made this class into the best class in the school. And the last thing I want is something like you around so I'm gonna see that you go back to whatever filthy dump you first crawled out of. I'll make you so miserable that you'll crawl to your horrible mother begging her to take you away.'

As he rabbited on, I thought, I don't have to listen to this and taking aim, I spat straight at the mouth that was saying it.

And knew I'd gone over the top again, that there'd be trouble, trouble, trouble all the way. So get out of here! What was I doing here among these *aliens* anyway? No, no, no, no, no – let me get away! Magnus

was towering above me, shouting for Mrs Flint,
trying to wipe his face, trying to grab me, so I dodged
under his arms and shot round the desks, heading for
the door into the corridor and out of school. Somewhere behind me, among the noise, I thought I heard
Beany call my name, and it warmed me so that a
feeling of freedom swept over me. Up, up and away –
through the streets – then down to the river and the
Joker and together we'll run and run for ever, over
the hills and far away. Through the playground and
along the pavement, the ground moving under my
feet . . .

I don't know whether it was Sean or Striker who
brought me down. But it was Magnus who got us
back to the classroom. They dragged me, feet trailing,

because I wouldn't walk. It didn't hurt, then. That came later. The class was standing as they hauled me in and dropped me in front of Mrs Flint's desk.

'Go back to your seat, Minty. Leave that boy alone!'

'He's hurt, Miss. Oh, they've hurt him!'

'There's the buzzer. Outside, all of you. Quietly now. We mustn't disturb the other classes. Yes, Mark Saunders, you must go too. That is a very naughty boy, so leave him alone. Go on, all of you.'

They went. I heard them go.

'Stand up, Owen Hardacre.'

I lay still. Why should I get up? What difference would it make to me now? I'd gone past caring. For it was all done for. Dad, I did try a bit. I did some nice work. (And I made two friends, I think. One's a bit of a cripple and one's only a girl, Dad, but they're OK.) I just can't take the *reading* and *him*, Piranha Face, together. Have I got to go on trying? Can't I just pack it all in? Give up, Ferret Hardacre, Useless Git.

'Can I do anything to help, Mrs Flint?' I heard Magnus say. He was still there.

'Yes, get him to his feet.'

No way! I got up, taking my own time. At last I faced her.

'Owen Hardacre, listen to me. I'M NOT HAVING DISGUSTING BEHAVIOUR LIKE YOURS! DO YOU UNDERSTAND ME? ANSWER ME!!!'

She shouted. There she stood, with her golden hair and blue eyes, *shouting*. Her voice blasted my brain. I lifted hands to my ears to keep out the cruel edge. Why was my world filled with horrible sounds? Don't, don't.

'LISTEN TO ME. YOU WILL BEHAVE WELL. YOU WILL NOT BEHAVE LIKE A WILD ANIMAL.'

Quickly she turned and wrote something on a piece of card. She took my fingers and forced them to follow the letters.

'Read this: "WILD ANIMALS SHOULD BE IN CAGES".'

There was a squiggle of blood from a graze.

'That's one reading method, of course,' someone drawled from the doorway. It was that teacher who read stories, Mr Merchant.

'You'll mind your business as I mind mine,' her voice whipped.

'I came to fetch Magnus for cricket practice. You *are* the Captain and need to organize it, Magnus.'

'Mrs Flint needed me, Sir. Sorry.'

'Come along, then. Excuse us, Mrs Flint.'

'Just a minute,' interrupted Mrs Flint. 'I want *him* to apologize to Magnus for spitting in his face.'

'Ah.' Did Mr Merchant's face flicker for a moment? No, it was dead pan.

I put my sore hands behind my back and said nothing.

'Say sorry.'

I did not.

'Mrs Flint, I really must take Magnus now. There isn't much practice time and we've a match tomorrow. Please excuse us.'

They went.

She and I were alone. And I was scared. I've said reading scares me, and Dad in a black mood, but she terrified me more.

'If you had apologized, I'd have let you off and you could have gone outside. As it is there is no alternative but to punish you.'

I had to place some chairs, backs inwards round a

table and sit in it. The wild animal notice was put in with me.

'What have I got to do?'

'Do some copying.'

'I'm no good at it.'

'Just copy one of these.' She pushed a book at me. 'Understand. *All I want is for you to behave well.* Remember that. *Behave well.*'

'What about my dinner?'

'It'll be sent along later.' And she left.

There was a long silent time. I put my head on the desk and tried to sleep, for I felt very tired. But sleep didn't come. I was hurting, aching now. I snivelled a bit. I wanted to put my arms round the Joker.

A whispering outside the window – kids playing; other kids – more whispering came from below the high window, miles off the ground. Ouch, a bump, a howl of pain. A grown-up said something. Quiet again. Then footsteps. And again, coming cautiously. Sh-sh-be-careful-giggle-giggle. The door opened, and a face came round it, dark curls, eyes like saucers, a big grin: Minty, and behind, Beany, worried, anxious, panda face. My heart raced. Someone had come. Minty ran, Beany limped over.

'I've got some crisps and half a bar of choc and an apple for you. In case she tries to starve you into goodness. Oh, your poor face. I'll bathe it for you.'

'No leave it. Let me eat this. I *am* starving.'

'WILD ANIMALS . . .' Beany began reading. 'Whatever's this? Why, wild animals aren't best in cages anyway, so it's a load of rubbish. What's the book?'

'I'm supposed to copy something out of it. But I

37

can't read it.'

'It's the *Book of Psalms*. Here, Owen, I'll copy one for you.'

'Your writing wouldn't fit. And call me Ferret.'

'Listen to this,' said Beany, opening the book.

'I am weary of my crying: my throat is dried: mine eyes fall while I wait for my God. They that hate me without a cause . . .'

'That's you, Ferret. But we don't hate you. You stood up to Magnus. I've wanted to do that all year. No one stands up to him nowadays. Minty tried. She told them she'd tell Mr Merchant. They're all right when he's around and last year they didn't do much but this year . . .'

'. . . I shouldn't have warned them. They threw stones through our windows at home and my mother had one of her funny turns – then Sean and Striker beat me up. Magnus watched and Ceefax laughed . . .'

'Doesn't anyone try to stop them?' I asked.

'The teachers don't know what they're like.'

'My mother thinks Magnus is a nice boy,' sneered Beany. 'Little does she know.'

'But the teachers must know . . .'

'Things happen to kids that tell. Two left last term. No one wants to risk it now. And it's nearly the end of our last term. So we go along with it.'

'I think they're up to some racket,' I said.

'Oh, yeah – they always are . . . They take money off little kids or kids on their own.'

'Shush,' Minty said. 'Somebody's coming. Let's hide.'

She shot behind a big wooden cupboard, Beany lumbering behind. But there wasn't room for two.

Minty giggled as they squashed together.

'Beany, I didn't know you cared.'

'I don't. Shut up.'

The door opened. Mrs Flint came in.

'How are you getting along, Owen?'

She stopped in front of me, blue and gold and pink, princess in a Grimm fairytale, very grim to me. I held my breath.

'Has anyone else been in here?'

I didn't answer. I couldn't answer.

'Look up, when I speak to you. Has anyone been in here?'

I looked as thick as possible. She gave a big sigh. Then she marched across the floor.

'Mark Saunders! Mark Saunders! I don't know *what* you're doing there, but come out NOW! And whoever's there with you!'

Chapter Six

FRIGHTENED PASSENGER: *How often does this sort of plane crash?*
AIRLINE STEWARD: *Only once, sir.*

I sat in a little room. This rotten day had already lasted for ever and here I was waiting for the Head-teacher to come and test me. What more could a kid want? Miracle, a miracle, please. Just a small one would help.

Mrs Flint had told a dinner lady to clean me up and feed me. Minty and Beany had to stay in the class-room and write lines.

I've had more tests than you've had hot dinners so I wasn't too worried about *them*. I could only do badly. Things couldn't be any worse than they were already, I thought, which only goes to show how wrong you can be. In the end it was Mr Merchant, Sir, who came. Chief Sir was seeing people, he said. But he didn't start testing me.

He peered at my face, asked me what sleep I'd had last night and what I'd eaten for breakfast. This sort of thing can make me really stroppy, but now I didn't mind and found I was telling him about Dad and his paintings and his black moods, and how to keep out of his way then, and about all the schools I'd been to, moving about the country as he tried to find a place which he liked for his painting and that he was OK if you knew how to manage him.

But my mother couldn't have found out how as she left just before I was six.

'You must have been starting to read then,' he said.

And then he asked me about the Joker and said what a terrific dog he was. Looks after you, I expect, he said, and then I told him what the Joker was really like, a softie and a coward, but don't tell anyone, I said.

'OK,' he grinned. 'What's it like not being able to read?'

What could I say? 'All right. I don't know any different, do I?'

'Is it difficult in shops or reading signposts and things when you're out?'

'I manage.'

'Do you notice colours and shapes and things like that a lot?'

'I suppose so, but how can I tell?'

'Yes, of course. It's me being awkward, asking silly questions. Don't worry, Owen.'

'I don't much. Only sometimes, Sir. And then I think, what about my reading?'

We sat quiet a moment.

'It's a good school here, y'know, when you get to know it. You won't be here very long since your class goes to one of the secondary schools at the end of term, but I hope you like it. Of course, you've only just come . . .'

'I came on Monday afternoon, Sir.'

'Yes, into our story. We were lost in it when you turned up. There was a unicorn – like me to read you a bit?'

He turned and took a book off the shelf and he read to me.

When he'd finished we sat for a bit, then I said I wouldn't mind being able to read that on my own. Then that's what we'll aim for, he grinned at me and slapped his knees.

'Huh, well, you don't look in first class shape to me so I'm not testing you now. Tomorrow morning when you're fresh would be the best time. Now, would you like to stay in here for a bit? You don't mind being on your own?'

I shook my head. Anything rather than that class.

'What would *you* like to do? Apart from going home, that is – help yourself to any books or magazines in here.'

'I'll draw you a picture if you like.'

'I should like that. What do you need? Felt tips, acrylic paint?'

'Just some paper and a pencil. Oh, and some charcoal if you have some . . .'

'I'll send some. Then I'll come for you later.'

He turned at the doorway.

'By the way, it's not a good idea to spit, however much they wind you up.'

'How did you know he wound me up?'

'He was in my class for a year. I know him quite well. No spitting. Remember.'

'No spitting.'

And I meant it.

I drew the leat and the ruins, hidden and mysterious behind the trees, the girder bridge and the old, broken water wheel.

And then I drew something I didn't know I knew was there, just showing through the leaves, two unbroken windows with tatty curtains in them.

Lionel snored. Dad painted. The falling-down house where time stood still smelt of oils, turps. The Joker leapt all over me. The kitchen was full of empty bottles, dirty glasses, cans, ashtrays full of butt ends (yuck and double yuck).

'You're late,' bellowed my dad.

'No, I'm not – I got a lift back with my friend, so I'm early, there!'

He didn't listen. He wasn't interested in what I'd done if it didn't concern him.

'Well, get a move on. You paralysed or somethin'? Clear this lot up and knock some sort of grub together. Oh, and do something about that dog. Hasn't been out all day. Get moving!'

'Get stuffed,' I said and, grabbing the Joker's lead, ran off into the sunshine on the quay, and past that to the leat where nobody goes.

And walking along there, or in Beany's case limping a little, came Beany and his mother.

'I didn't expect to see you here!' he said.

'It's great. I like it.'

'Oh, I'm so glad someone does,' his mum cried, beaming. 'I used to bring Beany and his sister Jane when they were little, but we haven't been lately because he's been ill . . .' she stopped. 'Sorry Beany, I promised, I know – but what I was going to say is that Beany's father says they're going to develop all of it, all this, and build offices and shops and a King Arthur leisure centre here. Here! Where we used to

see a kingfisher – oh, I can't bear it – it's terrible. Soon, there'll be nothing left!'

'What d'ye mean, Mrs Saunders?'

'There'll be no wild places left in England. No Wild Woods with Badger's House in them. Nowhere wonderful and strange. The whole country will be one Heritage Park with asphalt paths and castles made of breeze blocks and notices saying "Keep Off The Grass" and "Toilets 10p a pee"!'

'Mum,' muttered Beany, embarrassed. She took no notice.

'And your dad – he's an archaeologist,' she said to me. 'They've given him a dig here and he's pleased because he thinks they'll find something interesting . . .'

'Skeletons,' put in Beany. 'Skeletons are brill. Like

the ones he found in front of the cathedral, then they covered them all in again. I'd like to find skeletons . . .'

'Oh, the dig's all right,' said his mum, 'it's just that it's these awful people doing the developing who are funding the dig. So he won't protest because he wants to find out what's there. Then they'll cover up all the discoveries and build more useless offices and olde gifte shoppes.'

'Oh, Mum,' said Beany. 'Owen can't follow all that.'

'I can. And I think you're right, Mrs Saunders. They won't knock down the waterwheel, will they?' We were standing opposite it.

'Probably. And put up a plastic one. It's enough to make you want to get on the City Council, to do something about it.'

Beany offered me a crisp just then and I couldn't get it down fast enough.

'You hungry?' she asked. 'Come on back and have supper with us.'

'Oh, yes, please. What about the Joker?'

'He can have some as well. Come on!'

I suppose I should've guessed Beany's mum would live in one of the grand old houses perched above the red cliff that drops down to the quay. It wasn't like any home I'd been in before. I don't go in grand houses much. From Beany's room you could look down on the river and the estuary and the weirs – it's down to the sea that-a-way, he said, and oh, I liked that. Peering out of the window I thought I could see our falling down house. Yes, it's near, he told me, and there's a quick, secret way to your bit from here, down steps and a narrow alley between two high walls, it's too steep and overgrown for me just now, though I'll do it when I get better, but you can use it tonight when you go home, only don't go yet, it's early. He was talking very quickly and had spots of red on his cheekbones.

Dozens of books and models, stamp and fossil collections, engines and toy cars and a model steam engine filled the room, model aeroplanes, jigsaws, everything you can think of, cassette player, tapes and a Walkman, oh, and exercising machines – I have to practise on those every day, he said, sometimes my sister helps. I'd met his sister Jane downstairs, pretty, with a boyfriend. She smiled at me.

'You look like James Cagney in the old gangster films,' she said.

'More like a ferret,' said Beany.

Beany had got a lot of musical instruments as well, as I said, everything, and just for a moment I was jealous – then I looked at his worried panda face and his weak legs and I stopped feeling jealous. What was the point?

I recognized the cover of the book Mr Merchant read to me and took it down.

'I liked this,' I told him.

'I'll read some to you – OK? That is, if the idea doesn't give you the screamers.'

'OK.'

So he read, and then he played its tape on his cassette player and I tried to follow in the book, but couldn't make much sense of the squiggles.

'He doesn't read it as well as Sir,' I said but then we were called to eat. I'll say this, it was all fab, brill, but my casseroles are better. All the same, the ice-cream pud beat everything.

Aferwards we watched the portable telly in his room, which was great as I hadn't seen any for ages, ours being bust, oh, I don't know when. Dad hit it one day in a black mood, when it wasn't showing the right things for him.

I left at last. Down the steps and the narrow way. Beany was right, a smashing short cut between high walls, nobody about. Looked out for Magnus and the Meanies, but the coast was clear. Maybe they didn't know this path.

I slid in like the Invisible Man with Joker the Invisible Dog, not wanting to encounter Dad on the rampage.

The kitchen was tidy. Dad and Lionel were drinking tea and playing chess.

'There's a hot pasty for you in the oven,' he said to me. Full of casserole and ice-cream, I ate the pasty. Anything to keep Dad in a good mood. Besides, there's always room for more and I secretly gave half of it to the Joker.

Chapter Seven

A crack on the head is what you get for not asking and a crack on the head is what you get for asking.

Morrissey & the Smiths

I woke up feeling good and wondering why. Then I remembered yesterday evening. I had cornflakes and a bacon sarnie for breakfast and exercised the Joker before going to school, where it was gonna be OK, I thought, the worst over.

And this feeling grew stronger when I saw Mrs Flint had put a new set of paintings and drawings on the wall, all very neatly mounted (I know about that kind of stuff from Dad) and my water wheel picture was there. Minty said it was fantastic. Mrs Flint didn't get that excited, but she said Mr Merchant had given it to her as it was a good attempt, and it could go up with the others.

But Beany didn't turn up.

'He'll be ill again,' Minty said. 'Sometimes it's the aches or high temperatures, like flu.'

After Assembly, where Minty shared a hymn book with me and showed me some of the words, I went to the little room again and Sir did a lot of tests with me, then took me to Chief Sir for some more. I was more scared than I'd thought I'd be and when I got back to the classroom at playtime I was knackered.

The early sunshine had turned to pouring rain and though some kids went to the hall, most stayed in the classroom with books and games and drawings. I flopped down by Minty in a corner.

'Isn't anyone with us?' I asked Minty.

'You mean in charge of us? Oh, that's Penelope and Magnus, they're the class prefects.'

'Listen, everybody,' Striker said, banging the teacher's desk.

'I want to collect money for *our* present to Chief Sir,' went on Striker.

'My mum's given it to Mrs Flint,' said somebody. I didn't know all the names yet.

'You still have to give to our own present. Come on, hand over.'

He and Sean started to go round the class with a couple of Sellotape tins, and coins clinked into them. Striker came to us in the corner. Sighing, Minty handed over five pence.

'More later,' said Striker. 'Now you.'

'I haven't got any.'

'Don't give me that. Hand over.'

'I tell you I haven't got any.'

'He says he hasn't got any,' shouted Striker to Magnus.

'That's interesting,' said Magnus.

I braced myself, waiting to be bashed. But I wasn't bashed. Instead, Magnus whispered in Sean's ear. Sean turned to the newly mounted pictures and tore two off the wall – not mine, I noticed. Then he took a purple felt tip and scribbled on two more.

Minty's face looked agonized.

'What's going on?' I asked.

'You should have promised them something – oh, no!'

'Why on earth should I? If I give anything it'll be to the proper fund.'

'Don't you understand? They'll have you now.'

'How can they? Oh, I'm off. I'm not staying here.'

'It won't make any difference. It's too late – I should have . . .'

I couldn't follow her at all.

Ceefax had fetched Mrs Flint.

'He did it, Mrs Flint. He did it, Mrs Flint. When he came back from his tests he was so mad he did *that*, Mrs Flint. Look. He was like a wild animal. We couldn't stop him.'

He pointed to me.

I couldn't believe what was going on. Was I going crazy? And then it clicked. But surely – surely the whole class wouldn't . . .

'Owen Hardacre,' called Mrs Flint. Her voice made me afraid, made me shiver. 'Come here and give me an explanation of this.'

'But I didn't do that. He did. He did it,' I pointed to Sean.

'Come out of the corner! And tell me why you did this!'

'I DIDN'T DO IT. I DON'T WRECK PICTURES! Look, there's mine.'

'Oh, we know you'd leave your own alone. Oh, yes. Typical. You just wreck other people's work, don't you, boys like you, mindless vandals.' Her eyes blazed, her hair bristled.

'*They* know I didn't do it. *They* saw Sean tear up the pictures.' I waved at the kids in Class 4F.

But they were turning away, backs to me.

'I didn't see anything.' 'Don't ask me.' 'I was reading.' 'I've only just come in.' 'We was playing draughts.' 'I was busy.'

'Penelope,' I called to her desperately, a name I knew. 'You saw Sean tear the pictures. Not me.'

'I can't say who did it. I was organizing the Maths resources shelves,' she replied.

I swung round from one to another to meet blank faces. Magnus came forward.

'Mrs Flint, we know who did it. And I'm very sorry. I'll tidy them up if you like. I'm sorry we didn't keep him in order better, Mrs Flint. I'll try not to let you down again.'

Minty stood up, chin trembling, her face dirty grey. She said,

'Mrs Flint, Owen didn't do it. It was Sean, like he says. Because Owen wouldn't give any money to Magnus's fund.'

The words dropped like stones into a deep silent well. Everyone listened. Everyone watched. But I was coming up for air. Surely, surely *now*, we'd get the truth. But Mrs Flint only shook her head.

'Minty, poor Minty, when are we ever going to get you out of the habit of telling lies? We know you're kind and you want to help Owen, but we do know what you're like, don't we, dear? And it doesn't do any good in the end. Now sit down and read your book while I deal with this wicked boy . . .'

'BUT SHE'S THE ONE TELLING THE TRUTH,' I shouted, nearly going out of my head, Minty crying.

'Be quiet! You've done enough damage. You and I are going to see the Headteacher. The rest of you get on with your work until I get back.'

*

The Headteacher watered a nasty looking plant with a teapot and listened to Mrs Flint. I opened my mouth to tell him the truth, then shut it again for there was no point in saying that I hadn't done it, that I liked pictures, I'd been brought up to rate them the best things since the Pyramids and even if I didn't go that far, I'd never vandalize them, but I was in the land of Grown Ups where nothing makes sense. I'd never make Chief Sir and Mrs Flint know I was telling the truth so I wasn't even gonna try. She explained to him but before he said anything there was a knock on the door and Mr Merchant came in.

'Oh, sorry,' he said. 'Still, you're the ones I wanted to see. I finalized the results of Owen's tests and he's well above average in intelligence. Good, isn't it? All we have to do is sort out this reading block.'

Mrs Flint's voice made the Antarctic feel like the tropics.

'Then there's even less excuse for his non-existent reading and his anti-social behaviour. And I should like to point out that with a large class like mine, I can't cope with this child as well as everything else for the remainder of the year.'

'You may go, Owen. Just restrain yourself for the rest of the day,' said the Headteacher. 'I'll consider your case further.'

'But I haven't done anything wrong yet today!' I cried as I went, not meaning to, but driven to it.

Mr Merchant left with me.

'What's going on? Did you mean what you said? And what are you supposed to have done?'

I told him.

'You see, it's Magnus. All the time,' I said at the end.

'Well, that's your version, Owen. The class has a different one, you say, and you're new and Magnus has been at the school for some time. Is there anyone to speak up for you?'

'Only Minty. Beany's away.'

'I see. You'd better get back to the classroom.'

No one but Minty spoke to me as I went in. Not that I wanted anything to do with that snivelling bunch of cowards, lower even than Magnus and the Meanies, bullies and liars that they were. Almost – almost, I felt like telling my dad about them, but telling Dad never did any good. He'd probably wreck the classroom and me with it.

Minty was scared of what they'd do to her now. After school, she said miserably. I told her I'd stay with her, but there's only one of you, she whispered, black curls drooping, no smiles.

But about five minutes before the end of the afternoon, the door burst open.

'Please knock . . .' said Mrs Flint, looking up, as a figure appeared in a tinsel wig, a bus driver's jacket, mini-skirt and wellies. In one hand she carried a bag. It split as it swung against the door and out cascaded onions, nuts, oranges, books and a couple of bottles which banged together, splurging brown sauce and red wine everywhere.

'Half a league, half a league, half a league onward,

Into the valley of death rode the six hundred!' she sang.

Mrs Flint stood up, her face looking as if all her worst nightmares had walked in. Minty hid her face in her arms and groaned. I jumped up. I'm good on broken bottles – I can clean up without 'em cutting

me. Practice with Dad's done it. And this woman was the nearest thing to Dad I'd seen in a long time. I was half way through getting rid of the mess with a newspaper when I guessed who she was.

'THIS IS OUTRAGEOUS,' shouted Mrs Flint.

'No, it's Mollie,' answered Chief Sir, appearing from nowhere. '*Get back in your places, children.* Owen, you're doing a good job there. Go on. Mollie, you must have sold a poem.'

'Yes, yes . . . to the *Observer*. Alleluia!'

'Alleluia, indeed. Congratulations! I'm always pleased when one of my old pupils does well. Minty, where are you? Your mother has sold a poem. Isn't that splendid? Mrs Flint, I think on this high note we can dismiss the children. Good afternoon, children.'

'Good afternoon, Sir,' 4F chorused.

Somehow he then manoeuvred Minty, her mum

and me out of the room, leaving the rest of the class with Mrs Flint.

We walked out quietly behind Chief Sir and Minty's mum, as he saw her to the gate.

'Don't you dare say anything! My mum's the cleverest, best person who ever happened, so there!'

'I wasn't saying anything! You should see my dad. Now, he's really crazy.'

She turned a quick cartwheel out of the blue.

'Here we are, all grand with Chief Sir! Magnus and the Meanies can't get us now!'

She was the right way up, a good thing, when Chief Sir turned round to speak to me.

'Ah, by the way, Owen, tomorrow you will rejoice in the presence of a minder.'

'What, Sir? Sorry, Sir?'

'A minder, boy. You're going to have a minder. Just like that TV programme I regret I used to watch regularly.'

Chapter Eight

JUDGE: *Do you plead guilty or not guilty?*
MAN IN DOCK: *What other choices do I have?*

They got Minty.

She knew they would. I met her on the way to school and she was quiet and miserable. When I asked her what's up, she said they'll get me.

'If they hit you, I'm going straight to that Mr Merchant.'

She looked at me with eyes like black sad pools.

'You don't even begin to know. It'll be in some way you've not even thought of. That's how they operate.'

'You make them sound like the Mafia. Kids aren't that clever.'

'Magnus is,' she said and wouldn't talk any more.

Beany hadn't turned up and my minder had and Minty was in a state of terror. It didn't feel like an all-in-fun day to me. Almost I thought of mitching but Dad's threats had been heavy. Besides, Minty had said, 'Don't go. Stay with me. Don't stay away.' I didn't know she was psychic.

'Cricklepit Combined School dates back to 1665 when it was established by the Dean and Chapter in a small schoolroom in the churchyard. The school building was relocated in 1803 and extended in 1854 and 1895.

'The pupils have a rich variety of backgrounds. Some of their surnames are in the earliest recorded history; some local families have come recently from Vietnam, China, Pakistan or the Caribbean; some parents are postgraduate students or lecturers at the University; some cook the best fish and chips in the city. The School is still Church of England but its children are of many faiths . . .'

My minder was reading this to me, pointing to every word. To her the words made sense but not to me. She was a fat little lady called Mrs Malpas.

'I'm your shadow,' she said. What was I supposed to say? She would help me with reading in class and stay with me at playtimes and lunchtimes.

'More like my prison warder,' I said.

'Don't be like that,' she answered.

So there she was seated beside me while Mrs Flint began a new project, the History of the School. She'd talked to us about this and asked the kids to bring any old pictures, photographs, mementoes of earlier times, especially if their parents had been at the school. Any old school books would also be welcome – to be returned of course, and so on.

Since I hadn't even heard of Cricklepit Combined a week ago, I didn't feel I had a lot to offer. Still, I made a folder for my bits and pieces and my minder helped me with reading and copying. I was bored stiff at first, then I got caught up in the drawing of the school I wanted to put on the front of the folder, the tree and the school and kids under it. I quite liked that and didn't immediately get up to vamoose outside when the bell went – in any case, walking round the play-ground with Mrs Malpas wasn't exactly gonna be the thrill of the year.

'You and I will go outside together,' she said.

'What a giggle.'

'If you think . . .' she began and I never got to know what I was thinking, for a batty looking kid called Jason rushed in. I was starting to know their names by now.

'Mrs Flint, Mrs Flint, somebody's stole it!'

His eyes stood out on stalks.

'Jason, just calm down and tell me sensibly what's the matter.'

'I brought some money for you – for Chief Sir – and my mum put it in an envelope with my name on it in case I lost it, but I forgot and left it in my anorak in the cloakroom and it's gone. Somebody's took it. Somebody's stole it, Mrs Flint.'

'Bring me your anorak, Jason. Stay in the class-room, everybody.'

A murmur went up.

'I want to go out to play.'

'Why can't he look after his money?'

'I didn't take it.'

'Nobody said you did. It'll be somebody out of 4M poking about in our cloakroom. Or that ferrety new kid.'

I felt like smashing in the face that said that.

'You didn't take it, did you?' asked Mrs Malpas.

'Course not. You've been wi' me all the time, remember?'

I think it was then that I began to get the idea.

All 4F was brought back in and told to sit in its places

while Mrs Malpas took over Mrs Flint's desk as she searched the classroom. At last she came back in, frowning.

'I'm very, very angry. Jason, if you'd remembered to give me the money at the beginning of the morning this needn't have happened. But even worse is the thought that there might be a *thief* in this class.'

The eyes sparked, the hair bristled, she started to shout. Shrinking small into my seat, I tried to pretend that I couldn't hear, that this wasn't happening.

'I'll begin with Owen Hardacre. Come up to the desk and bring your work tray with you.'

'It couldn't be Owen, Mrs Flint. I've been with him all the time since he came,' put in Mrs Malpas and got a glare.

But of course I was clean – no money on me. She came to Minty's tray about half way through. The money still in its envelope was in there, pushed to the bottom of all her stuff. I remembered Ceefax and Sean up and down all morning, Mrs Flinting and fetching things. I stood up.

'She didn't take it. I know she didn't take it. Magnus fixed it . . .'

Mrs Malpas pulled me down on my seat.

'Don't talk like that. Just keep quiet. Saying things about Magnus . . . Why, he's always looked after Jason. You don't know anything about this school.'

'Oh, I do, I do,' I cried. 'I know Magnus is wicked . . .'

Mrs Flint said, 'Sit down, Owen Hardacre. Find him some work to do, Mrs Malpas. Minty, stand by my desk. The rest of the class may go out to play now.'

'It wasn't Minty. Minty,' I shouted. 'I *know* you

didn't take it. I'll get him. I promise.'

'Owen Hardacre, be quiet or I'll send you to the Headteacher!'

We were both shouting now. Minty drooped by the desk, smiles and sunshine gone for good.

'I'm very disappointed in you, Minty.'

'What do you expect with that mother?' Mrs Malpas said, seated beside me. I'll get you too, I thought.

'I liked her mother. Looked human, which is more than most people do here,' I hissed at her.

'Just you be quiet if you don't want to be reported.' So I sat silent. Watching smiling Magnus walk out on air.

After play Mrs Flint went on reading more about the school eighty years ago, ready for the project.

60

'Very strict discipline in that school: you wouldn't dare be late, you wouldn't dare answer back. If you were late you had to stand by the side of the class so that all the children could see you. And you knew you were going to have the cane for being late.'

She seemed to be looking at me, so I stared down at my folder. Mrs Malpas sat beside me.

'Someone from long ago had written: "It was a big classroom in the senior part of the school and probably we were doing sums – it wasn't called maths then. Mrs Webber used to teach the senior girls and she would say, 'What's three nines?' 'What's ten fours?' And if you didn't know the answer, you had to write it out fifty times to make sure you knew it".'

Mrs Malpas must have been getting some ideas 'cos when Mrs Flint had finished, she made me write out certain words twenty times each.

'I still shan't know them tomorrow,' I said. 'So it's a waste of time.'

'I think you're one of the most awkward boys I've ever known,' she told me. 'Get on and write out those words.'

After a while she said, 'Just be thankful you weren't here in the olden days, Owen.'

'What's the difference? In this class, anyway.'

'You're a rude, ungrateful boy.'

'I bet they used to say that kind of thing in those days, as well.'

I hadn't seen Minty since the morning.

Chapter Nine

BRENDA: *Mum, is it true that we're descended from apes?*
MOTHER: *I don't know, I never met your father's family.*

And that day was Friday. I'd been at this school almost a week . . . and for ever.

I ran home, cooked sausage, eggs and chips for Dad, me and Lionel, not thinking about doing it at all because my head was crammed with thoughts and feelings. Then I saddled up the Joker and set off along the quiet alleyway between the high walls up to Beany's house, so full of what I was going to tell him that it was only when I'd rung the doorbell that I grew nervous. They mightn't want to see me, might tell me to go away . . . After all, I wasn't Number One in the Best-Loved Kid Polls.

Beany's sister opened the door and grinned all over her face.

'Hi, kiddo,' she said. 'Come in. Will he be glad to see you. Talk about fed up. Here, I'll take the pooch, you beautiful wolf, you . . .'

The Joker rolled over on his back and waved his paws in the air. She laughed and rubbed his chest. He showed her he was ready to die for her there and then, the two-faced animal.

'What a fraud!' she said.

'No, just a Joker.'

Beany had come out to meet me. He looked terrible, but cheery.

'I tried to ring you . . .'

'Lionel's been cut off. He never pays any bills.'

'I'm glad you've come. My brain's aching with thoughts going round and round in the same track all the time. Like, am I going to end up growing into an eight foot freak? I don't much fancy being an eight foot freak, not even if it means I can go to the circus every day.'

'Well, it's not much fun being my size either. Everybody gets on to you . . .'

'How's it going? Come on. Give . . .'

We went into his room and I told him about what had happened during his two days away and hot rage steamed up inside me again so that I couldn't stay still but marched up and down like a robot.

'They got us. First me, then Minty. And there's nothing we could do. Nothing. And I haven't seen her since Mrs Flint took her somewhere. I wanted to talk to her. I thought you'd know where she lives.'

'Yeah. I'll come too if my mum'll let me but the trouble is I've been ill again and I'm supposed to rest. Rest! When I want to get Magnus before I die!'

I was shattered. He looked so strange standing there on his stork legs, shaking his fists at a Magnus who was probably gambling away Chief Sir's retirement fund at the amusement arcade . . .

The two thoughts colliding in my brain almost knocked me out.

'You're not gonna die, are you?' I managed to get out first. He put down his hands and collapsed on to a chair.

'Oh, I dunno. It's just that nobody knows what's really wrong and when I'm on my own a lot, I get to thinking awful things. But when I feel better and can get around, I'm OK and I know they'll cure me.'

'Yeah, yeah. I know they will. You'll get better, I know you will.'

I wanted to cry – I hurt inside, which felt very strange because wandering round with Dad had stopped me feeling anything much about anyone except when once I'd been scared the Joker had gone for good. I didn't like this feeling at all, so I latched on to the other idea that had taken a tour round my pea brain. Anything to change the subject.

'Beany – listen. Forget about dying. Please. It's Magnus. I think he's a gambler. At least, every time I've gone past the amusement arcade, he's there on the machines. And the others. But it'll be Magnus who decides if that's where they're going. Now, say he can't stop it . . .'

'Compulsive gambler, you mean.'

'Yeah.'

'He'll need money. You always lose in the long run, my dad says . . .'

'You mean Chief Sir's private fund for Chief Sir's present. Our own private one from *us*?'

'I thought it sounded phoney at the time.'

'But how is this going to help us?'

'I dunno yet, but it's something, isn't it? We gotta find out all we can about him and then tell Chief Sir.'

'Oh, Magnus has always been the Boss. He's big and tough and he's lined up the toughies to be his special gang. The teachers like him.'

'Mr Merchant?'

'Not sure. He keeps him down, but he did make

him captain. He's the best at football and the best at cricket. I used to stand up to him but then I became ill and I was always away, so . . .'

'I still don't believe it. All those kids saying it was me . . .'

'They didn't *actually* say that. They said they didn't see anything.'

'Came to the same thing. Tell me more about Magnus.'

'His dad's rich . . .'

'Surprise, surprise.'

'He owns a lot of the shops and the nightclubs and property round here. His mother's all right. She's on the PTA and my mum knows her. That's why *she* thinks Magnus is OK. He was gonna go away to school last year but his mother's soppy about him and talked his dad into letting him stay another year . . .'

'Yuck.'

'What about the rest? Would anybody come in on our side? Penelope?'

'Her dad's the Mayor this year. He's big on the Council. Friend of Magnus's dad.'

'He would be. Is there anyone? Besides Minty?'

'A kid called Duncan, he's OK. Silent kid. He keeps out of trouble but he doesn't go along with Magnus. And then there's Peter Singh – Magnus gave him a rotten time and he hates him, so does Gary Slade. If they thought there was a chance they might come over. Su Martin used to be a good kid, and Kelly Davis, but he threatened them and there hasn't been a squeak out of them since. And there's Minty. Nobody can squash her for long . . .'

'They're doing their best.'

'Why, what you got in mind, Ferret?'

'Nuthin', nuthin'. It's just I gotta do something. I can't stand the lies and it being so unfair. I never did anything wrong. Neither did Minty. And that horrible big . . .'

'You want to see her? Shall I ask my mum if I can go out? Oh, that's terrible. I bet you just clear off outside whenever you want. Whereas me – I've got to ask Mummy,' he said in an incy-wincy baby voice. 'But', he growled, 'if I could just get better and do in Magnus, I'd be happy.'

'If I could read and duff in Magnus, I'd be over the moon.'

Suddenly we shook hands. Beany nearly fell flat.

'Not much of a fighting gang, are we?' he grinned.

'Go and ask your mum . . . And I tell you what – if she lets you out, let's see if we can spot Magnus in the amusement arcade without him seeing us.'

Beany's mum said he could go out for an hour.

'Don't let him tire himself out,' she told me. Beany glared.

'Leave Wolfie with me,' Jane said. 'I'll have him.'

He rolled over on his back and waved his paws at her again, the traitor.

Minty's house stood in a square of funny little houses all turning to each other wearing aprons of flowers, garden gnomes and cats. Beany banged a devil knocker on an old green door. Two of the window panes were filled with cardboard.

Faces peered and curtains flapped.

'Gone away. Back in the morning,' said the old geezer next door. 'I've got to feed 'er cats. Tiger,

Geoffrey and Beano. All ginger toms. Never cared for ginger cats meself. Come to think of it, I've never much cared for cats. I'm a bird fancier, meself.'

He shook his head at us and stomped inside.

'Dad's started the dig,' said Beany. Let's take a quick look.'

The leat path was tricky because of broken bricks and stones and Beany's legs. Right at the far end under the high, red wall, sandy holes had appeared beside the path. A drainpipe and two cables looked up at us.

'No skeletons,' Beany sounded disappointed. 'I'd've liked skeletons. Just holes. Looking like bog holes to me.'

'Maybe skeletons later.' I didn't care a lot one way or the other but if skeletons made him happy – let there be skeletons.

The leaves hid nearly everything now, but not the waterwheel which hung sad and still and I wanted to go over to it but I thought it would take Beany ages, so I kept quiet and we wandered back on the quay.

Spy-time.

'D'you think they'll be there?' asked Beany.

They were. We watched cautiously from the entrance.

Beany hissed, 'The gang's all here.'

And they were. While chart music played, lights flashed blue, green, yellow, red, and fruit machines blared space sounds, Magnus, Striker, Sean and Ceefax put in coins, pushed and held buttons with great concentration.

'Look at what they're putting in. Where do they get

all that from?' Beany whispered. 'Loadsamoney.'

'I dunno. Chief Sir's present fund probably.'

'But they're not winning *at all*.'

'Look, you see I was right, Beany. Let's go now. Before they spot us.'

He wouldn't stir.

'Let's go,' I said again. 'Beany – it's time to go – your mum said . . .'

No use. Beany wasn't listening.

Walking very straight for him, and when he's straight that's about five ten, even if it's the thinnest five ten ever, Beany went over to Magnus and the Meanies.

'Hi,' he called out. 'Give me a go.'

They fell back, staring.

Dear God, please look after all idiots tonight, I prayed as I followed.

Beany fished money from his jeans pocket. Just

look at the lolly these kids have down here tonight, I thought, and me, little, poor, a baby bird out of its nest with big black cat Magnus waiting to pounce. They'd made Beany a space but I was ignored and I didn't mind. I just covered his back. Music grew louder, the lights flashed, we were on another planet. Me, I was scared. They couldn't do anything inside, but later ... outside ... But not Beany, he didn't care.

'Any luck?' he asked.

Magnus shook his head. 'Not paying out at all tonight.'

Beany pushed in a coin. We watched, mesmerized.

A triple bar fell in on the first reel, followed by a second, then a third. Every light flashed on, on, on. Fire brigade sirens blared and coins cascaded down, down, down, like Niagara.

'You jammy ...' shouted Striker.

Beany was grinning from ear to ear.

'You have to have some luck somewhere, some time,' he laughed. 'Even me. Come on, Ferret, kid.'

He started to fill his and my pockets, stopping to give Magnus, Striker, Sean and Ceefax each a coin.

'Have those on me,' he said and headed limping for the exit, me close behind.

Jane and the Joker greeted us. There was orange juice and salad rolls and nuts, Beany stuffing it down like one of the starving.

'Hey, what's got you?' she asked.

'I won. I won. I won something. Here, for you.'

'Are you sure? Gee t'anks. Howdja get all this? Robbin' a bank?'

Beany told her.

'Gambling? Mum'll have a fit!'

'Don't tell her, then. Besides, you don't have to worry. It was all for purposes of investigation.'

'What on earth is he talking about?' she asked me. I didn't know what to say.

'We'll tell you some time, ole girl,' Beany said, and then, 'Where's Mum?'

'She's decided to get involved in local politics. So she's gone to get herself selected as a candidate for something or other.'

'Good. She'll have less time to worry about me then.'

'Yeah. Thanks for the cash, Beany. But you won't get hooked, will you?'

''Course not. It's a mug's game.'

Up in his room, Beany divided the rest of the money out between us. I tried to stop him, but he said he felt good for the first time in ages and not to spoil it, so what was I to do? Besides, I don't get much. Dad's generous with *his* drinking pals but he doesn't think I need anything.

At last, worn out, Beany lay back on the bed, very white, the panda eyes showing up clearly.

'Magnus's face,' he murmured and grinned to himself.

'Magnus's face,' he sang. 'Magnus's face. When I won all the loot, that *they'd* put in, Magnus's face – oh, the look on Magnus's great horrible face!'

'He'll make us pay later.'

'It was still worth it.'

I got up to go.

'Kiddo?'

'Huh?'

'It's great. That gambling stuff.'

'NO! NO! Don't get caught on that, you idiot.'

'I'd've thought a kid like you, being streetwise – is that the word? – and all that – not like me, never going out, Mummy's boy – would've liked a go . . .'

'Look. That's it. Because I'm streetwise, as you call it, I wouldn't. My dad says gambling's for idiots and he knows I might spend 10p but no more . . . You've probably had all you'll ever win, Beany. Don't start gambling.'

'I was only joking,' he muttered, rolling over and hiding his face.

I left, not sure whether he was or not.

I could feel the coins in my pockets – I'd got money to spend. And it was Friday. Super-duper. Brill, great, fantastic. No more school till Monday. And I'd got through a week of this new place. Beany was sure he could help me learn to read, he said. And somehow Magnus and the Meanies could be sorted out.

Friday night. Everything's possible. All the world's there, Friday night, hooray. What would I buy with all this lovely lolly?

Chapter Ten

'Knock! Knock!'
  'Who's there?'
'Armageddon.'
  'Armageddon who?'
'Armageddon out of here!'

They waited for me in the quiet alleyway. Just how
stupid can you get? Very. What made me think they
wouldn't know it? Like Beany, these kids had lived
here for yonks. They'd know every bit of the place,
every hideout, every nook and cranny.

They waited at a bend where branches spread over
the walls on both sides, a tree tunnel, quiet, dark.
And the secretness of the lane that'd made me think
it safe was really its danger. Nobody was gonna trot
along here to give me a helping hand, no Chief Sir
taking his wife for a walk would save me. (Reckon I
ought to give something to the real present fund for
last time – especially if he'd just come along again
now.) No hope. Magnus and Sean, Striker and
Ceefax were lined up against the walls, two on each
side. The joke was I'd let the Joker go. He'd been
tugging, wanting home not far away (only a million
light-years) so I let him off the lead.

I turned and ran back up the steep path. Hilarious.

I could hear Ceefax laughing like a drain.

Magnus stood over me as Sean and Striker held me. Magnus smiled. Beautiful set of teeth.

'Hello, Ferret.'

'How's your trousers?' giggled Ceefax.

'Not ferrets he's got in them, is it, kid? It's money. Our money. Just hand it over and we won't hurt you . . .'

'Much,' put in Striker.

Some idiot called Ferret spoke.

'No, it's Beany's money. He won it.'

'We're not taking *his* money, we're taking yours, 'cos you ain't got no right to it, Ferret. Come to think of it . . .'

'. . . he's got no right to anything,' giggled Ceefax.

'How right, right, right you are. Striker, get the money.'

I went bananas. I shouted and yelled, kicked and punched. But Sean put his smelly hand over my mouth as Striker emptied my pockets, tearing them as he went.

'Not his face,' ordered Magnus. 'I want him pretty and unmarked – so I can do this . . .'

Sean moved his hand, I opened my mouth.

Magnus spat into my face. Ceefax fell about. It dribbled down. I couldn't wipe it off. Sean clamped back his hand.

They were throwing everything down on the path.

'Ceefax, pick up the money.'

Down on his knees he sorted out the coins from the old string, and peppermints, bit of comb and the pebbles and dead leaves. The coins he gave to Magnus. Sean and Striker held me still so I could watch. I tried to bite the horrible mauler as Striker then turned

me and tore off my back pocket to check if any money was left in there. Magnus counted the money.

'It's just under half of what Beany stole off us. It'll do, I suppose. Come on, let's go.'

'I wanna hurt him. Just a little bit,' Striker wailed, pushing his face near mine.

'No. Leave him. Let's get back to the machines.'

'Let Striker have his little bash,' giggled Ceefax.

'No. We're going.'

Striker's parting punch doubled me up. By the time I'd straightened up, I was alone.

I tried to creep in without being seen.

Dad was just off for a Friday night jar with Lionel. I didn't want to see his face. I didn't want him to see me.

'What you bin up to?' he shouted. 'Where you bin? What you done to that uniform I've just bought? I'll thrash you, I will. D'ye think I've got money to burn? Just you wait . . .'

'Oh, come on, Joe – come on. Leave the kid. Give him a good hiding in the morning. Don't spoil the evening . . .'

They argued until at last . . .

'Oh, OK,' muttered Dad and as they blurred off into the evening, I blurred off into Lionel's camp bed.

In the night it collapsed. Too knackered to put it back together, we just lay together, the bed, the blankets and me. For what did it matter? What did anything matter?

Chapter Eleven

'Why did Robin Hood rob the rich?'
'Because the poor didn't have any money!'

The bell rang. It rang again and then again before it got through to me. Go away. Sometimes that bell works and sometimes it doesn't. It was working now. Better get up before it wakes Dad and murder breaks loose. Somehow I got to the door and opened it.

Minty stood there.

'D'you always sleep in your clothes?' then, 'What happened?' and, 'They got you, didn't they?'

I just stood there holding the door and I knew she could see inside where one of Lionel's mates was sleeping it off on a sofa – well, the remains of a sofa.

She didn't say anything, just grabbed me and pulled me on to the pavement.

'No shoes,' I managed.

'Get them quick. No, Joker, you can't come. We've got three cats.'

The bathroom had seaside postcards pinned all over one wall and reflecting back in the huge mirror above the bath. Flowers seemed to walk in at the window and on the wall beside it was a poem (I could tell it was a poem by its shape) surrounded by a drawing of a girl in a tower in a forest. She stood by a window with long plaits hanging down to a witch below. I didn't know about the poem but the drawing was brill, I thought, stretching my legs in the hot water and investigating bruises. Not too many. Magnus had seen to that, but I'm not grateful, I thought, as I wallowed. Lionel's only got a shower and half the time it doesn't work.

Breakfast was as good as the bath and they left me alone to eat it. As I did, I looked round the room. It was jam-packed with all brightly painted things, curiosities and funniosities, shabby and tatty books and flowers everywhere and old dolls and toys on chests and tables and pictures and clowns and battered trains and trays – everywhere covered, everything coloured, a grown-up's toy shop. Three ginger cats watched me eat. They're why we couldn't bring the Joker, said Minty.

Minty and her mother came back in before I'd realized they'd gone out. I'd been so caught in looking at things and talking to the cats.

'Here,' said her mum. 'These should fit. I can mend your blazer and the shirt but not those trousers.'

'But you can't buy me . . .'

'Yes, I can. Don't argue. You'll only lose.'

'But Dad'll kick up . . .'

'Your dad's not taking much care of you. So I wouldn't worry about him too much . . .'

'He's all right really. It's just he only . . . thinks about his pictures.'

'His pictures?'

'He paints. He's packed in his job so he can paint. We've moved about a bit while he tries to . . .'

'Find himself . . .'

'Yes. How d'you know?'

'Oh, I know. I've been trying to do that for years but I keep getting away from me. Now why don't you two wander while I clear up a bit . . .'

'I don't want to meet Magnus . . .'

'Quite understandable. I could go for years quite happily not meeting Magnus. What a revolting name – it suits him.'

'What about the one you gave me, then, Mum?'

'Oh, you'll understand that later. I got it from a book called *England Made Me*. You might read it one day. . .' she said to me.

'Not very likely. I can't read, you see.'

'Oh, my dear lad. Well, we'll soon cure that . . .'

'Everyone thinks that. It never works.'

'We'll see. Look, kid, you've got the palest face I've ever seen. Minty – I know, let's dig out some money and you and Owen go to the beach. On the train, Owen. It's wonderful. Much better than in the car. Not that we've got a car. How could I afford one? Have you been since you've been here?'

'No.'

'Off you go, then. Wait, I'll have to get some money out of the marigold teapot, the electricity bill money, but we'll worry about that later. It's summer now, so who cares? Push off now. It's going to be a beautiful day. Get back for tea, OK? From now till tea time, is out of time time. Oh, Lordy Lordy, how terrible, sometimes I don't feel I'm up to this poetry lark. I'll take up jogging instead and git healthy.'

'That'll be the day, Mum.'

'Here's the money. Clear off, have fun, keep out of trouble and if you catch a whiff of Magnus, blow this.'

She threw Minty a whistle.

'That's the one I keep for muggers and rapists. But take care. You could whistle up the wind or an ancient terror from the sea. See you, kiddos.'

'See you, Mum,' said Minty.

'See you,' I muttered. Women, especially mothers, troubled me terribly, and not at all in the way things like Magnus or not reading or Dad troubled me. She called out,

'Change those trousers first. And leave the blazer and shirt. Wear this tee shirt . . .'

An out of time day. The train ran by the estuary. It looked like a toy train but Marines from a barracks got on and little kids with buckets and spades. The tide's in, said Minty, and there's a heron, look, he always sits on that post. The sand stretched for miles and it

was easy to get past all the people to where the spaces were big and lasted for a long way. We paddled in the water but it was cold. Minty collected shells and made a pattern in the sand. We bought ice-cream and take-aways, and climbed down cliff steps to a rocky shore, a world away from the sandy beach with the mums and little kids and coloured umbrellas. I watched the boats and the surfers, another different world. And the dogs. Running over the sand, they reminded me of the Joker and I missed him, but last night he'd deserted me, left me alone.

We bought a beach ball and played with it, then had a go on the kids' tin-pot train, and a wander round the Aquarium. Sometimes I felt peculiar being with a girl, but mostly it was comfortable, no hassle with Minty, sometimes we talked, sometimes we didn't, and we never once mentioned school.

In the end we had to run for the train. Neither of us'd got a watch and we forgot the time. The tide was out on the way home and the estuary was another place.

We ran back to the square, where the cats slept in the sun and the old geezer next door watered his flowers.

'I like it here,' I said to Minty.

'Coming down next year. It's in the way of a development scheme,' said Minty's mum, sitting on the doorstep with a book and a cat on her knee.

'Oh, call me Mollie,' she said. 'You can't go on saying "Minty's mum".'

She'd made something called lardy cakes for tea.

'Sheer murder they are. Kill you as soon as look at you. Go on. Cut one open, pile butter and strawberry jam in it and you'll never smile again. You'll be too

80

full and happy.'

She was right. I ate nine or ten, I lost count.

'Don't want to go back to Lionel's,' I said, much later.

'Understandable,' said Mollie. 'But you're not, anyway. I visited your dad this afternoon and you're staying tonight and tomorrow night.'

'What – what did he say?'

'Who? Your father? Oh, he was all right. I've seen him around. Fixed him a hangover cure and he told me he'd sold not one but two pictures. He's on top of the world. So you're all right.'

'Oh – fantastic. Oh. Is he mad about the clothes . . . ?'

'Relax. Everything's settled. Here, have a drink of this . . .'

'Watch it – it's home-made elderberry. Dynamite! Don't give him that, Mum . . .' warned Minty.

'Just a drop. It'll send him to sleep . . . he needs it.'

They talked as if I wasn't there, but I was too laid back to care. She gave me a little glass and listen, she said to me as one of the cats, Tiger, climbed on my lap. She started to read to me and sounds washed over me, beautiful they were. Then she seemed to be reading out of an old, a very old book, reading the story that goes with the drawing in the bathroom, and then another and another and I'd heard them all long ago somewhere and then one even more long-ago story about a witch and a cat and I wanted to cry terribly because of something, something . . . but lads of twelve with dads like mine, hard men, don't cry, they've got to be tough to fight Magnus and Striker and all the rest. And still she sat reading while I felt sleepy and strange but Minty was smiling and the cat purring and at last, still holding the cat, I stumbled over to her mother and put my head in her lap and let the story wash over me like the sea ebbed and flowed over the sand and the rocks and the pattern of shells that lay on the beach.

Chapter Twelve

'Why don't cats shave?'
'Because eight out of ten cats prefer whiskers.'

Mrs Malpas waited for me at the school gate. But Beany waited too, and Minty walked beside me because I'd come from her home, not Lionel's. Magnus and Co. were conspic. by their absence but they couldn't really touch me, could they, not with Mrs M. around? She stopped me getting up Mrs Flint's conk but, I'd only just realized, she stopped *them* getting up mine.

Beany came round to the side where she wasn't and talked over Minty's head.

'Did you spend your money on anything good?'

'No,' I answered at top volume. 'Rotten Magnus and his horrible friends mugged me on the way back from your house and took the lot . . .'

'No,' shouted Beany, 'not all that lovely lolly . . .'

'. . . and vandalized all his clothes . . .' put in Minty.

Mrs Malpas looked splatted.

'What d'you mean?' she spluttered. 'Magnus, indeed. What are you all up to . . .?'

'Me, Mrs Malpas?' asked Beany, all innocent. 'I never get up to anything. You know that. But I'll get

83

that lot, I swear . . . Tell me. What happened?'

'They waited for Ferret, bashed him up and took the money that Beany won and shared with him. Just like always,' said Minty.

'But Owen looks all right . . .' said Mrs M.

'My mother mended his clothes and Magnus doesn't let Striker go for faces.'

Mrs Minder had gone very pink and was breathing fast.

'I've never trusted you, Minty,' she said at last. 'Nor that mother of yours . . .'

'And what about me? And my mother?' asked Beany.

'That's different . . .'

'But we say the same things. And I'm saying that I'm raging mad at them stealing that money. *I* won it and I wanted Ferret to have some, not Magnus and his Mafia . . .'

'Beany . . .'

The whistle blew and it was time to go in. Mrs M. stalked in with me, a very funny look on her face. After dinner money etc. she edged her way up to Mrs Flint's desk and whispered in her ear, so that we couldn't hear what she was saying but you could tell what it was about by the glances she shot at the class.

'Not now, Mrs Malpas. I'm really too busy to deal with matters of that sort. Children, I want to tell you more about our new project. Listen carefully, I shall . . .'

'. . . say this only once,' put in Beany.

Mrs Flint opened her mouth and shut it again.

'I don't want to repeat this over and over again. We all know the Headmaster is leaving and we want to give him a good send off, don't we?'

Sounds off from class 4F.

'Open Day this year will be dedicated to him. You know that the Headmaster has been here for a long time, has served the school well. We shall be doing a Walk Back Through Time, so the parents can wander through the school where memories of times past await them. We've already made a start with some of our work on the history of the school this week. Parents and friends of the school will be lending photographs, pictures, books, music, records, clothes and costumes, trophies, certificates etc.

'In our class we shall have a Day in the Past. A Day in 1913, actually . . . We shall practise the day before and do it again for the parents on Open Day.

'Then there'll be a presentation to the Headmaster. I hope you won't forget to bring a contribution so that we can buy something splendid. I wanted you to have time to think about all this. Now we are going to continue with our Maths as usual.'

We got stuck into Maths, Mrs Minder very fidgety and irritable.

'That's not right.'

'Yes, it is.'

'*There*. Look *there*. You calculated that wrong . . .'

'No, I didn't. *You* can't do Maths.'

'Could we have less noise, please?' Mrs Flint called out, making Mrs M. turn even pinker as she got up to check the answer.

'You were right,' she muttered as she sat down again.

'And we're right about Magnus and his gang,' I whispered. 'Minty didn't steal that money and I didn't vandalize the paintings.'

'Mrs Malpas, take Owen into the corridor and work with him there.' Mrs Flint's voice was as stony as her name.

The corridor was draughty and uncomfortable, with people trekking to and fro all the time. We sat glaring and talking.

'I don't like this job very much . . .'

'Well, give it up then. I don't need a minder . . .'

'I need the money. My husband's an invalid . . .'

'Sorry about that, but I need you like I need a hole in the head. I'm not wicked. I'm not even very naughty – Dad knocked that out of me. I just get mad when people wind me up or tell lies like Magnus did over me and Minty.'

'You've told me all that . . .'

'Well, listen again. It's time somebody did at this school.'

'It's a very good school. Or was till you came.'

'The school's probably OK. How would I know? But there are two things wrong wi' it – Magnus and Mrs Flint – and I land both . . .'

Chief Sir was standing over us. I didn't know how long he'd been there.

'Owen, I should like to have a word with you in my office,' he said. 'Mrs Malpas, a prospective parent is waiting in the hall. Perhaps a cup of coffee?'

Chief Sir watered his nightmare plant from a teapot and hummed a tune as I waited in – no, not terror, I'd gone beyond terror – sick nothingness. I wasn't here, it wasn't me. What was wrong this time? Had Magnus thought up something else? I waited and waited. He seemed to have forgotten me. Then he said,

'Oh, sit down, boy. We mustn't waste time.'

86

He handed me a folder.

'There's your reading programme in there. Mr Merchant and Mrs Flint have specifically tailored it for you.'

'Oh.' I tried to look as if I knew what he meant.

'Now since you appear to object most forcibly to any child helping you with your reading we thought it best for you to work with Mrs Malpas.'

'I – wouldn't mind . . .'

'What wouldn't you mind?'

'Beany. Helping me.'

'We'll see.'

He sat down at his desk facing me, making his hands into little steeples.

'Ahum.'

We waited.

'Originally you were placed in 4F because it's less crowded than Mr Merchant's class, 4M, the parallel one. But two children are leaving from there and Mr Merchant has expressed a readiness to have you. Would you care to move? We should not then require Mrs Malpas except for lessons involving reading.'

He waited, while I thought of lessons with Mr Merchant, Sir, and no more Magnus, *no more Magnus*, no more Mrs Flint, no more minder, perhaps even a laugh now and then . . .

'Well, child?'

'I'll stay where I am, Sir.'

'Oh. That's interesting. May I ask why?'

'I can't leave Beany and Minty, Sir.'

'Mark and Minty – that's Mollie's daughter. She had a reason for giving her that extraordinary name, I seem to remember.'

'The name's in a book, Sir.'

'Yes, so it is. Very well-read is Mollie. And we'll have you well-read too, Owen. We've got about six weeks to do it in. Oh, tell me just why you want to stay with 4F.'

'They're my friends and I don't want to leave them with Magnus and the Meanies.'

'Magnus and the Meanies? Now that *is* interesting. Tell me more about these – er – characters.'

What should I say? I opened my mouth and shut it again. Where to begin? This was the moment! Yet the idea alarmed me – could I do it? Would he believe me?

A knock, the door opened, the secretary poked her head round.

'That prospective parent is going to leave, she says, if you don't see her soon, as she can't wait for ever, and she's got four children, Top Infants, Lower Juniors – where the numbers are low, Sir. Can I deal with Owen?'

'He can go now. We'll have another little talk at some future date, Owen. Goodbye.'

My knees trembled as I followed the secretary back to Mrs Flint's classroom and the silence hanging like a fog over it.

Me and Mrs M. sat in the Library on our own with a cardboard box full of cards and pictures, boxes of words, notebooks and the programme file. On the top lay a book called a Spelling Dictionary but I couldn't know that until she told me. Beside us was a computer. And a video.

'Somebody's gone to town on you,' said Mrs M. 'I hope you're worth it.'

Mr Merchant walked in with a pile of paperbacks.

'I've even brought some books,' he said. 'Just in case we forget what it's really about. Lots of jokes in that one. To cheer you up when the going gets tough. Right, Mrs Malpas, are you ready?'

Chapter Thirteen

WOMAN AT DOOR: *I'm collecting for Barnardo's.*
FATHER: *There's four kids here you can have!*

After lunch Beany gathered up those kids he thought were really on our side, Duncan, Peter Singh, Gary Slade. Kelly Davis came along with Minty.

They came because Beany asked 'em and I got an idea of the kind of kid he'd been before he was ill, when he used to stand up to Magnus.

We got into a corner on a couple of benches. Mrs Minder came with me, so I said I'd push off so that she wouldn't hear what they were talking about.

'Why don't you join us, Mrs Malpas?' grinned Beany. So she did. It didn't take her long to get near to blowing up.

'I don't want to listen to all this!' she cried. 'It's just a pack of lies!'

'What, all of us telling lies? exclaimed Beany. 'Let's get it straight. Magnus and his gang bully kids, even the little ones, they take money off them, they frighten them. Magnus is a *thug*, a *baddie*.'

She stood up.

'I'm going to report you!'

'Yeah – do that! *Please*. Tell Chief Sir. Tell Sir. Tell Mrs Flint if you dare. Let's get some action!'

She sat down again, slowing down.

'Suppose I do. What'll happen to me? I work for his mother in the morning before I come here. And I need that job. I don't want to lose it.'

We stared at her as she carried on as if we weren't there.

'Sean's family live next door to us. He's got a very nasty temper, has Sean's father. You wouldn't want to get across him. My husband's got a weak heart and can't stand rows.'

'It's up to us to tell Chief Sir,' said Beany. 'All of us.'

'Just like that?' asked Minty.

'Not me,' Gary said, moving away. 'No way.'

Peter Singh murmured, 'They haven't hassled me for yonks. *And* I'm in the cricket team. With Magnus. Sorry.'

He followed Gary.

Kelly smiled. 'Me, I gotta go now. Mrs Flint wants me to sort out the Art area.'

Only Duncan stayed, saying nothing.

'What about you?' asked Beany, a bit flatly.

'Me? Oh, I'll kill him one day. But I'm not telling tales to Sir.'

'You always were a loner,' Beany said.

'Still am. But if you work somethin' out let me know. I'll be there, cheering. See ya, Ferret, see ya.'

Beany, Minty, me and Mrs M. sat there.

'I'll keep my eyes open for you if you like,' she said slowly. 'Kids crying and so on. Grown-ups don't always notice what's going on.'

'Thanks,' Beany said.

'Gym club for me,' called out Minty. 'I'm late . . .'

'I might as well do my bloomin' exercises,'

grumbled Beany.

'Let's go over those words again,' said Mrs M. to me. 'You remembered a lot of them last time.'

'Yeah. Yeah.'

After a bit: 'That Minty's a very strange girl. Mother's a witch, you know,' said Mrs M. as we worked our way through a list of words with 'short vowel sounds', and then,

'You know all these. Let's go on to the next lot. I'm surprised,' she added.

'Not half as much as I am.'

That night I wandered to the leat with the Joker, now friends again. He'd missed me and so had Dad, at least that's what he said. He was in a heck of a good mood, pictures selling now and some bloke suggesting he should have an exhibition if he could get enough pictures together – not that they'd need that many, some of Dad's canvases are pretty huge, stacked up in Lionel's attic which stretches all over the top of the house.

As we ran along, I watched for Magnus and the Meanies 'cos I did that all the time now, and I remembered they still thought the Joker was a Rambo-type fighting machine, not just the silly old softie. I had a destination in view – over the old bridge to the derelict buildings behind the summer-thick leaves. The first had wrenched-off doors, floorboards missing, windows like broken teeth, a dark, smelly, filthy place, frightening, spooky. The next the same. But the third was the one I must have photographed in my mind, not knowing I was doing it till I drew it in the picture for Mr Merchant. It was all in one piece, windows unbroken, old white curtains hanging, flight of wooden steps almost hidden by bushes and old plant pots leading to an upstairs door. The door below was solid – not wrecked like the others. I pushed it open and went in.

Bits of carpet lay on the floor, and in the corner stood a bed – no worse than mine at Lionel's – with blankets on it, and a chair, a table with a candle in a candlestick, a pile of old tins, books and boxes. Through another door into a kitchen with an old gas stove. A saucepan stood on it, a couple of milk bottles on the floor, a brown sink with an old enamel bowl in it and a tap. A brown thread of water trickled down when I turned it on.

Someone had lived here – and not so long ago either. The Joker ran round sniffing. The air smelt dusty but clean. The place was gloomy because of the trees but not spooky – not like the others.

A noise outside. I crouched down, holding the Joker still. Voices came nearer. Perhaps just some people going for a walk or to look at the excavations further along. When they'd gone past, I'd leave – I didn't want to hang around in case I ran into Magnus and the gang. But I guessed I'd be safe as he found it hard to tear himself away from the amusement arcade. The night they'd followed me was because of Beany's money.

The voices died away. I settled back. This place was well hidden. You wouldn't notice it much. We sat for a while, the Joker and me.

Better get back to Lionel's. Homework waited. This Reading Project was high-pressure stuff. Didn't want Mr Merchant on my back.

'We'd like this breakthrough before you leave for the Secondary school,' he'd said, 'but don't worry about it.'

I wasn't. I'd stopped worrying about reading. Somebody else had got it lined up for me.

'Just do your best, Ferret.'

'He always knows kids' nicknames,' Minty told me. 'And the teachers'.'

No sign of Magnus as I ran back. He was quiet tonight.

He may have been. Dad wasn't. Hammer and tongs, Dad and Lionel were shouting, creating merry hell. The air was blue, Dad roaring like a bull, Lionel screaming about parasites, layabouts, spongers.

'. . . you cretinous, feeble-minded half-wit,' bellowed my father. 'What did you try to move that painting for? Why didn't you leave . . .?'

'. . . it was in the way. It's so big . . .'

'. . . have asked me! I've sold that one to old Masterson, loads o' lolly he's promised and you put your useless, great, ugly feet through the corner of it . . .'

'. . . took you in, you and that flea-bitten dog and that stupid kid . . .'

The Joker and me, we slipped away, the Joker whingeing 'cos Dad in a rage scares him. Where to go till it blew over? Not Minty's because of the cats and a bit late for Beany, he has to go to bed early, always moaning about it.

Back to the secret house. Stay there for an hour and slip back in when they'd calmed down and it was safe. That's the idea. I'd got enough money to buy some crisps.

I sat on the chair by the table – the Joker lying at my

94

feet – and waited. After a while I picked up one of the books and opened it – a paperback, some sort of teenage story, judging by the cover. I expected it just to be a jumble as usual but I could make out the shapes and patterns of the words better than I'd ever done before. I started to work out some words: I – and – but – ran – said – boy.

I couldn't stop. I turned over the pages, reading words here and there, short sentences. She was running to-wrasd – no, towards – me. The Joker snuffled and kicked his back legs, dreaming doggy dreams. He kicked his back legs again happily, chasing rabbits probably. I went back to chasing *my* rabbits, the words I knew in the story. It seemed to be a teenage love story, not that I cared, I just wanted to find words. 'I-dream-of-you,' – he said – 'I dream-of-you.'

The door opened. I nearly jumped out of my skin. The Joker leapt up and growled. A girl stood in the doorway, staring in terror at the Joker and me. I could hear her quick breath. And mine.

'Who are you?' she whispered. She looked just a kid.

'Who are *you*?' For one wild moment I'd thought she was a ghost, and I was as scared as she looked. The Joker solved it. This was a girl and he did what he does with girls. He rolled on his back and waved his paws in the air.

'Oh,' she dropped the carrier bag she was holding on to the bed. 'He won't hurt me, will he?'

'Not 'im.'

'Nor you. You won't. You're too little.'

'I'm strong, though,' I said, hurt. She didn't answer that but went on, 'I didn't think anyone knew it here but me.'

'I found it.'

'Me too. You haven't brought anyone else here?'

'No.'

'Do you think anyone else knows it beside us?'

'I don't know. I haven't lived around here long.'

'I want to stay here. Don't tell anyone, will you?'

'No, not if you don't want me to. But you're not staying here on your own!'

'Yes, I am. Camping out.' She's round the bend, she looks round the bend, I thought.

The Joker waved his feet again for her to pat his chest. She smiled a bit, I think, but it was hard to see for it was starting to get dark, and bent over him, and then I saw that she was pregnant.

I felt just as if somebody had punched and winded me.

'We'd better go. Come on, Joker.'

'You won't tell anyone I'm here. Promise.'

'But aren't you scared? Here on your own?'

'No, I stayed before. It's all right.'

'I can find somewhere for you, I think, if you're homeless,' I managed. 'A kind lady with three cats. And a daughter. They're friends of mine.'

'No. I want to be here. Just go. Don't tell anyone. Promise – cross your heart and hope to die . . .'

'Promise.'

''Spect I'll leave tomorrow.'

I pulled the Joker up and we ran home on powered feet.

I crept in, not wanting to see Dad and Lionel, which was easy as they were out. I crawled into bed but couldn't sleep as thoughts ate like maggots through my brain.

Chapter Fourteen

'It was a great disappointment when we realized
he was dyslexic. We thought he was studying Russian.'

James Bond had a girl friend. He `taught` her
everything he knew and so they never got `caught` .
One day they shot lots of people for robbing a bank, a
big `slaughter` . James's girl friend had a `daughter` .
She was `naughty` and loved to `laugh` .

Exwick Reading Workshop

Reading, reading, reading.

Mrs Malpas took me through the words. Mr Merchant heard me read every spare moment, sometimes his own stories. Word cards, software, typing, writing, scrabble with Minty, comics, adventure books with Beany. His mother got me in the reading workshop on Saturday mornings where kids worked quietly, no pressure. I liked it better than cleaning up after Lionel and Dad's Friday night sessions. The lady at the workshop said she thought I wasn't dyslexic but that I had a reading block. That's your head, said Beany when I told him – it's twice its usual size 'cos of all the attention you get.

'I'd hit you if you weren't so feeble.'

'What – you – your size! Don't make me laugh. You couldn't squash a flea.'

'I'm tough, even if I'm not very big. Look at that muscle . . .'

'A flea bump . . .'

'You've got fleas on the brain . . .'

Reading, reading, reading. Sometimes at the weekend Minty's mum read me strange tales from her hundreds of books. Sometimes boring, sometimes they made my hair stand on end. They made me feel weird, unpeeling me. I half liked it, half didn't.

I learnt to use a Spelling Dictionary, finding out

about sounds and syllables.

> One tap for **fun,**
> And two for **be–gun,**
> Three taps for **sta–di–um,**
> And four for **gym–na–si–um.**

I learnt, I learnt, I learnt, and the words started to jump out at me. I started to read things I didn't know I knew.

'You're so lucky,' said Minty's mum. 'All those books waiting to be read and you haven't started till now. Lucky Ferret!'

And I practised writing and learning to spell.

'You've grown a bit,' said Minty.

'He's still a PORG,' Beany grinned.

'What's that?'

'Person of Restricted Growth!'

'How can *you* say that?'

'That's why I can.'

I filled up with words while the school filled up with 'Days Gone By': pictures, photographs, maps, prints, mementoes, kids, teams, old school staff looking from another world.

One afternoon Sylvania School's cricket team arrived for *the* match of the season, the Derby. It was warm and sunny and the school trooped out to watch and cheer. I sat with Minty and Beany as Magnus made the best innings of the season, hitting four fours and a six. The Sylvanians were flattened, and Cricklepit Combined went wild, as they streamed on to the pitch, cheering and shouting, 'Magnus! Magnus! Magnus!' Penelope rushed forward and kissed him. So did some of the other girls.

'Didn't you do well?' I heard Mr Merchant say . . .

'Well played, sir,' cried Chief Sir, clapping.

In Assembly next day we clapped him again – at least the others did.

Mrs Flint hauled me out to the front of the class later as she gave a talk on 'good sportsmanship', while Magnus sat back in the class and smiled his piranha smile.

'You have to admit he's wonderful,' said my minder. Scrabble letters made a rude word I'd just learnt to spell. She flushed red.

'We could do without the likes of you in this school,' she muttered. 'He's a fine boy. You'll see how well he does at Sports Day.'

'Striker'll win the weight lifting, I suppose. And the baby bashing.'

'One more remark like that and I'll report you to Mrs Flint.'

I wasn't listening. I'd found I could read 'pneumonia' and 'knickers'.

'Mrs M. you'll need another job soon,' I said.

She was suddenly a *different person*, not the leader of the Magnus fan club. 'Owen, I don't know how I'll manage.'

'The Lord will provide, Mrs M. "Alleluia!" Minty's mum says that.'

'You are a funny kid. *Sometimes* you're not all bad.'

'Only half bad, like salmonella eggs?'

'Please work QUIETLY.' Mrs Flint rapped the desk.

School was busy. And at night I slipped out to see the girl in the old building. I sneaked food with me because she seemed to have run out of money. She was always pleased to see me but even more pleased to see the Joker. She'd throw her arms round him when he appeared, then he would roll over and wave his paws.

I didn't know what she did all day, though I knew she read a lot of paperbacks. When I asked her she said she was waiting. I kept thinking I ought to fetch Minty's mum to her but then each night she made me promise not to tell anyone but now she looked more like a ghost than ever. In the evening I'd take her whatever I'd been able to save or scrounge and she pecked at it. She liked ice-cream best. I kept thinking I must do something about her and each day I put it off.

Striker brought round a collecting tin for Chief Sir. I didn't argue this time. I put in money like the rest.

'Learning sense as well as reading,' leered Striker.

I didn't answer.

But to Beany I said, 'Magnus must be skint again. Gambling not paying off?'

Mrs M. had a funny look in her eyes.

'Little kid in the Infants crying. When I asked, he said Striker did it.'

Chapter Fifteen

'My dog has no tail.'
'Oh! How do you know when he's happy?'
'He stops biting me.'

Over the old girder bridge – jump up and down, catch an overhanging branch, the Joker leaping and lashing his tail, maybe he thinks I'm his squirrel. He'll chase me to find out, but I can beat him, beat him, beat him . . .

'Hey, Ferret, you're good,' – that's Minty.

'Bet you I can't do that. Look out, you nearly fell in!'

'Not me. Suckers on me feet like flies got.'

'I didn't know you were athletic . . .'

'And I can play the mouth organ . . .'

'Not here. The birds'll hate it. So will my dad.'

We're down by the leat to watch Beany's dad and the rest on the dig.

'Guess what, you two?' asks Beany.

'I don't know how to . . .' Minty answers.

'What?'

'Guess what. I can guess the time, Ferret's birthday, the name of your favourite rock group, but not what's what. My mum says I don't know what's what.'

'What?'

'No, what's what.'

While those two maniacs rabbited on, I hung upside down from a railing sticking out from the wall.

'Look at 'e thar, Minty. Monkey 'e be.'

'Always zed as 'e ware monkey.'

'Nay, nay, lass, that b'aint monkey, that be un verret.'

'Ah, un verret. Nasty critters, they . . .'

'Ah, very nasty.'

'Ferret?'

'Yeah.' I dropped down and joined them.

'Guess what.'

'You already said that, Beany.'

'Well, it's important for you to know this.'

'Git on wi' it.'

'Dad's excavating bogs.'

'Bogs.'

'Middle-aged bogs, loos, toilets, what 'ave you.'

'Never! Poor things. Didn't know they got middle-aged. D'you think they'll get rheumatism?'

'What?'

'You get rheumatism when you get old and middle-aged.'

'Minty, you're barmy.'

'I know. I like being barmy. Stops you being serious.'

'I meant,' said Beany. 'They were built in the Middle Ages.'

'No! Fancy!'

'Yes. A sort of Middle Ages public loo.'

'Oh.'

'Makes you think.'

'Thought it was all Roman down here. Or Anglo-Saxon. Or . . .'

'No, the loos are . . .'

'Middle-aged.'

'Shut up, you two idiots,' said Minty. 'I want to think.'

'You can't. You've got no think tank.'

'*Yes, I have.* Ferret, are you doing anything for Sports Day?'

'Me. No. What Sports Day? All I do is read, remember?'

'Next week. Lists are up. You sign on the one you want and they file you into the house list. I'm hurdling. It's all done in houses, you see. They like at least two from each house for a race.'

'Only time we use the houses these days,' Beany put in.

'I'm not signing. Why should I? What are your houses to me? I'm not even in one as far as I know.'

'I'll see to it. Old Flintbag and me are like this these days.' Beany wrapped one finger round another.

'No!'

My 'no' made *no* difference. Beany put my name down just before the lists were taken down so nobody would see it.

Sports Days, I've been to a few. Don't mean a lot if you're always on the move . . .

In the school it was Magnus all the way. Bets were he'd be Sports Boy of the Year, Penelope Sports Girl. ('Sexist', muttered Minty.)

And Beany signed me up. Pig.

Which was how I came to be jogging up and down on a coldish, wettish afternoon in a borrowed kit that was too big for me. Entered for the Obstacle Race.

'Well, high jump and long jump are out for you and you're a slow runner so it's the Obstacle. Lots of balancing,' he explained.

'It's the rottenest idea ever. Striker will probably break me leg.'

'Nobody'll get at you with everybody watching. Magnus is busy watching *himself*. He's got to get this one to be Sports Boy. Peter Singh's won as much as he has.'

'This is ridiculous. I hate you, Beany.'

'You can only come last. That's what they'll think, anyway. So you've nothing to lose.'

'If they damage me, I'll damage you.'

'Threat or promise? Go on. They're lining up.'

'As long as they don't break me legs . . .'

'Not easy here.'

'Striker finds it easy anywhere.'

'You gotta go now. Good luck, Ferret.'

I was alone (with the other competitors). I'm always alone. And scared. Think I'll drop out now. Sir walks along the starting line having a word.

'Good lad, Owen!' he says to me.

Shouts all around. 'MAG–NUS! MAG–NUS!' One or two 'PET–ER's get drowned in 'MAG–NUS! MAG–NUS! MAG–NUS!'

Noises, shouts, cheers, a hooter, whistle, a loud-hailer and Chief Sir shouting. 'PARENTS AND CHILDREN. THE VERY LAST RACE. AND THE MOST EXCITING! TWO HOUSES ARE LYING EQUAL! BLUES AND GREENS!'

'What am I, Sir?'

'Green, idiot. From yesterday.'

'As long as I know.'

'MAG–NUS! MAG–NUS!'

And I could hear Beany's voice shouting, 'BAG–PUSS!' and then 'PIG–NUTS!'

Shivers. Wish I was dead. Not raced since – long ago, before we started moving – why think of that now?

The Starting Whistle.

Hurdles first. Coming last, but over them now, clipped one, over the horse, over the box, somersaults on mat, balls into buckets – easy – climbing ropes on apparatus brought out specially, through tunnel – easy, easy – I'm gaining now – not last any more – long jump over mats – not good, dropped back again – trampoline, three bounces, better, skittles, only two in front of me now, Magnus and Peter . . .

'MAGNUS! MAGNUS! MAGNUS! PETER! MAGNUS! BAGPIPES! BAGNUTS!' and a girl's voice:

'FERRET, Come on, FER–RET' and more voices are joining in, 'FER–RET', 'COME ON THE FERRET!' They can't be calling for me, it's not possible.

The high fence – it's enormous to me – this is where I lose. Up – go on – up again and over and fall down and there's only the balance forms before the finish and Peter and Magnus are wobbling – it's hard after all the rest – and I run over, nippy and little, and it's the finishing tapes and Beany yelling 'BAGNUTS NO WAY! FER-RET!' and Minty throws her arms round me and holds me up and Mrs Malpas is holding up Beany and we are both gonna die, I think, and Peter Singh is shaking my hand and Duncan slapping my back and Kelly kisses me, and Peter Singh is second and Magnus third.

'Sports Boy of the year is Peter Singh,' shouts Chief Sir into the loudhailer.

Chapter Sixteen

'How old's your dad?'
*'I don't know. There were so many candles on his last cake
we had to call the Fire Brigade.'*

'What made you think you could get away with it?'
Magnus murmured gently. 'Nobody does that to me.'

'Can't take losing, eh?' I uttered as bravely as poss.
But it was no use. I was scared stiff. Having Beany
with us hadn't helped this time. Magnus's eyes were
strange and I felt sick inside. They'd dragged us
behind the trees. Help was far away.

Minty, Beany and me, we'd gone to look at the
excavations. We thought Beany's dad would be
there, but he wasn't.

Magnus and the gang were. They'd been looking
out for us.

'You lot have hassled me all this term and I've had
it up to here,' explained Magnus, as if it was the most
reasonable thing in the world, and this frightened me
badly. 'So I'm fixing you for good. Tell them what
you got there, Ceefax.'

'Solvents,' giggled Ceefax.

'Glue to the ignorant. You —— are all going to
have a sniff – a nice big sniff – and then tomorrow, I
shall report you to Mrs Flint. As Class Prefect, I'll be

doing my duty. I'd suspected you lot for some time. Always hanging secretly about here so we followed you and guess what . . .? You three all sniffing like crazy. Come on, let's start with you, Minty. Sean, you give her a really good sniff – Sean's an expert. Been flying high for ages, has Sean.'

'*Stop it*, you idiot,' Beany cried, while Striker held him. 'What you messing about at, crazy loon? That stuff can kill – specially if you force it on her like that. Kids have died! There've been lots of cases in the papers. Don't be a fool! What good will it do? What's the flaming point?'

He was talking furiously now, and I could hear his mother in his voice, but he was saying anything, anything to stop Sean.

'You can't really mind Ferret winning? You've won everything all your life – while he's had nothing. And what does a race matter? You can't win everything, Magnus. Someone's bound to beat you sooner or later. And does it matter? What diff—?'

'SHUT UP, YOU!'

Striker hit him hard in the mouth . . .

'That's the difference,' he snarled.

And Minty went bananas. Sean couldn't hold her as she struggled and shouted.

'Stop it! Stop it! Help! HELP! HELP! Come here! Somebody come – HE-E-E-ELP!'

She was digging in her pocket with her free hand. She found something there and pulled it out, then blew on her mother's whistle as hard as she could.

A crashing through the undergrowth – a hurtling – a grey and yellow body – a wolf – the Joker!

And following him came a great big bloke, arms

up, ready to take on anything that might be there.

'What the —— is going on here?'

The air turned blue and crackled as Dad loomed over us, six foot odd with flaming hair and beard.

'What —— —— are you lot up to? Owen, git talking. Fast!'

Minty threw herself at him, wrapping her arms round him.

'Stop them, stop them, oh, please, stop them for ever!'

Tears rained down.

'OK, OK, OK. Calm down. Don't you dare run off!' Ceefax was grabbed. 'Stand still. Don't move. I'll sort this lot out.'

Magnus rallied.

'Mr Hardacre – that's you, isn't it? Your son and his

friends are glue-sniffers. We've just found them,
With this . . .'

He pointed . . .

'No, no, no, it isn't true. He always tells lies. But
it's him, all the time. Please believe me. I'm not a thief
and I don't sniff glue and please, oh please,
somebody stop him!'

'She's hysterical. Just like a girl.'

'Sir, I'm glad to meet you. And I'm Beany. Your
son's friend. What Minty says is true . . .'

'What's wrong with your mouth?'

'He hit me. Striker . . .'

'I told you. Never faces,' snarled Magnus, and then
knew what he'd said. Dad was there in a second.

'I want to hear about this, so I think the girl is going
to tell me all about it. Joker, don't let them move! Go
on, girl.'

'She's called Minty . . .'

'Well, Minty. Talk.'

We all stood there while Minty told him everything, and the Joker managed to go on looking like a
wolf.

'We're off to see your father. No, don't argue. Just
take me to your old man. I don't care who he is, he
can be the President or Mrs Thatcher as far as I'm
concerned, it's all the same to me. We're going to see
him. All of us. If anyone tries to run, the Joker will
deal with them. Now, move.'

Across the quay Dad herded us, sheep with shep-
herd and his dog.

'They won't let you in.'

'You won't get past the bouncers.'

'My dad won't see you.'

He took no notice.

We stopped at the nightclub and entered the gloom inside. Magnus tried to run, but was hauled back. Minty grabbed my hand. The bouncers, if that's who they were, came forward, but Dad said something and a woman appeared who led us through doors and upstairs. Again Magnus tried to talk and was silenced, tried to run and had his ear grabbed.

The woman knocked on the door and let us in. Magnus's father stood by a fireplace on the far side of the room.

'What on earth?' he exploded. 'What are you lot all doing here? This is an intrusion. Magnus, what's going on?'

Dad was grinning. Teeth gleaming under the ginger tash, Dad starting to laugh. I know that laugh. Run for cover.

'Why, it's Greasy Reynolds! Old Greasy Reynolds! Fancy seein' you after all these years! Who's put on weight? And going bald! And who are you cheating now, you old rogue!'

Greasy Reynolds or Magnus's dad stared in horror.

'Oh, no, not you, Not you. I hoped I'd seen the back of you. Joe Hardacre, of all people. What are you doing with my boy?'

Dad told him. Loud and clear. It went on for some time while we stood and listened and Magnus somehow shrank and Striker and Sean cringed and Ceefax didn't giggle at all.

Beany sat down, suddenly shattered, his eyes shining.

'And why?' Dad turned to me. 'And why didn't you tell me about these – animals – before. I'd've stopped this stupid carry-on in no time. Owen, you never had any sense. It was all so simple . . .'

'We can see this now, Sir,' said Beany. I wasn't used to me dad being called Sir.

'Now, Greasy, your lad and his mates need taking in hand a bit, I reckon. Are you gonna do it or am I?'

'I didn't know he was bullying little kids and taking money off them,' muttered Magnus's dad.

'You should've —— guessed then,' roared Dad. 'Because that's what you did. Remember poor ole Fatty Sinclair? Tried to hang himself and couldn't make it. And I bashed you up for what you did to Mary – what was her name?'

'Parkin,' said Mr Reynolds gloomily. 'All right. I'll take him in hand. Magnus, you BEHAVE YOURSELF FROM NOW ON, D'YOU HEAR ME?'

Magnus nodded miserably.

'What about this lot?' Dad waved a hand over Striker, Sean and Ceefax.

'There won't be any problems. I employ their parents. There'll be no more trouble this term.' He sighed heavily.

'And next . . .'

'I'm sending Magnus to a boarding school.'

'And the best of British luck to it.'

'Is that all settled then?' asked Dad. 'I've got things to do.'

'Just a minute . . .' Beany said painfully. He looked shattered. '. . . there are a few things. Minty was called a thief when she wasn't and Owen a vandal . . .'

'. . . doesn't matter. I don't care, Beany,' I said.

'But I do,' said Minty, 'and then there's the money they took off Ferret . . .'

'How much?' sighed Mr Reynolds, but his eyes were black chips.

'I want my mother,' Magnus cried suddenly. 'And I don't want them to laugh – to tell me off at school. I'm Top Boy.' He crumpled up, weeping.

'Oh, it doesn't matter except for Minty,' I muttered, 'cos I felt awful watching him cry – but not Beany. He came out with . . .

'You're pathetic. You always were pathetic. That's why you've always had to bully everybody, to show off . . .'

'Leave it,' my dad said. 'Kid, you're right. But I don't want to hang about here all evening talking as I can think of better things to do. You lot had just better go to your teacher and tell all – or I'll turn up and do it for you. There, all settled.'

'Oh, no,' groaned Magnus.

'I don't care,' spluttered Striker. Sean's face was set, no tears, not like Ceefax, sobbing.

'That's right. Own up. Like the old days. Nothing like good old-fashioned discipline, I say. Did us a power of good, eh, Greasy? Made us what we are today, you a crook and me a failed artist.'

'Anything you say, Joe, anything you say.' Greasy sounded tired. Dad does that to people.

'I think your dad's wonderful,' crooned Minty. 'And you didn't tell us! I wish he was my dad.'

'Your mum and my dad would last for about ten minutes and then they'd be throwing things at each other.'

She wasn't listening. 'He paints. He's an artist.'

'And a bully, in his way. As bad as Magnus, really. That's why he could sort him out, I suppose.'

116

'You are funny. Come on. We've won. We can have some fun.'

Dad had told Mr Reynolds to take Beany home as he was very tired. Minty and me, we wandered over the quay, safe at last. But there was still something to do, something bothering me.

'Minty, come with me. Please.'

'Where?'

'I've got to get some grub from Lionel's and take it to somebody. Don't ask questions – just come with me . . .'

One of the best things about Minty is she doesn't make a fuss. She kept quiet as I grabbed some bits and pieces and a spare bottle of milk, and then we set off for the girl in the old building. By now it was growing dark.

'Minty, hurry!'

'I can't. I'm tired. What's it all about?'

'You'll see.'

We crossed over the bridge and into that strange little house. The girl lay groaning on the bed.

Minty ran over.

'Ferret! Ferret! She's going to have a baby soon. Soon! Nearly now. We've got to do something! Fetch my mother! Quick! Run!'

The girl grabbed my hand.

'Where's the dog?' she asked, and would not let go.

It was Minty who ran, and me who stayed there holding her hand while the pains seized her, then let go, then seized her again. I couldn't do anything else, she held on so tight.

'Is the dog all right?' she asked once. 'He's not here.'

117

'With Dad,' I said. 'Minty's gone for her mum. Don't be scared.'

'Don't be scared,' she echoed. I didn't know if she meant me or her. She'd never seemed all there. It didn't seem to make much difference.

Mollie and the ambulance arrived together. She'd rung immediately. And then there were people everywhere.

'I'll go with her,' said Minty's mum.

But it was me she wanted.

The day ended with me riding with her in the ambulance to the hospital.

Chapter Seventeen

KEEP OUT!

This Means <u>You</u>!

Reporters tried to get into our classroom to talk to Ferret but Mrs Flint kept them out. She got very angry and shouted at them. But they waited outside in the playground and got him after school when Beany showed them where he was hiding behind the Lost Property Box. Beany was falling about with laughing. He's getting a mean sense of humour now he's getting better. I used to think I'd like him for my boyfriend but not any more.

Ferret's picture appeared on the front page of *The Echo* under a headline,

ONLY A KID CARED

And there was also a picture of the funny place where she stayed hidden. *Back to Victorian Days* was written underneath.

Ferret keeps saying he didn't do anything, only feed her. Without his friendship she would've died, the paper said. Ferret gets very red and blotchy if you talk about it. It was the Joker she liked anyway, he says. *Only a little boy and a dog to save her*, it goes on.

I'm not that little, Ferret mutters. Crossly.

The girl has had a baby daughter and I've been to see her with Mum. *She* goes every day. They're staying longer in hospital than usual because the baby's extra small. Nobody knows her name or where she came from. She won't say. Ferret says it's because she isn't all there. But I think she is. She always asks after him and wants to come out soon to see the dog. My mum says she can stay with us till things sort out. I hope the girl realizes Mum is very bossy and will take over the baby completely. But perhaps someone will come forward to say she belongs to them. She calls the baby Rabbit. I told you, says Ferret, she's not all there.

He also said the reporters tried to find him at Lionel's, but landed Dad Hardacre himself – so instead of news about the Care Boy (Beany's new name for him) they found themselves having a preview (I think that's right) of his paintings, as his dad couldn't care less about Ferret or the girl. He's got Magnus's dad to set up an exhibition and a large advert went in the paper. Mr Reynolds paid for that as well, Ferret says.

Magnus and the Meanies are very quiet. Magnus doesn't look like a shark any more, he looks like a spaniel who has buried a bone and can't remember where. I feel quite sorry for him which makes Beany cross. Perhaps he does *not* have a caring nature, at least where Magnus is concerned. He says he wants to be a politician, so he won't need one. Just strength, that's all, and he seems to be getting that OK. He's also got very keen on the amusement arcade, though we try to stop him. He dragged us in there the other night, huh. No Meanies. Sean and Ceefax are getting treatment to stop them sniffing glue. Striker is going to karate classes.

I fancy Mr Hardacre no end, but so does Mum so that's no good. Mind you, they shout at each other rotten especially when they start discussing whether Art is better than Poetry or Poetry better than Art. If my dad comes back there'll be trouble but it doesn't seem likely. Striker keeps writing me little notes, but I throw them away.

Mrs Flint was ill after the news about Magnus which was all over the school in no time. I heard Mrs M. say, 'I told you but you wouldn't listen,' in *that* kind of voice, and soon afterwards the reporters turned up and then Ferret suddenly became the School Hero, Number One in the School Charts, what with the Obstacle Race win as well. Penelope started to talk to him but he just kept running away and hiding, so she turned to Beany instead. *He* couldn't get away. Ferret had to go and be clapped in Assembly. That's when Mrs Flint got ill.

One of the dinner ladies left. Mrs M. took her place, a good thing as I don't think the School Hero should have a minder (though it might be like the Queen or Princess Di, I suppose).

The fan club soon got fed up. Ferret kept reading to them. It gets pretty boring listening to a book you've read yonks ago but he's just got around to. But Ferret reading made the Wrinklies happy. Mrs M. said *she*'d done it, everyone said it was Sir as usual, and Beany said his mother claimed it was the Reading Workshop.

But I know. It was my mother, of course. She put a spell in that elderberry wine when she read the witch and the cat story to him. She says that was the one his mother told him the night before she ran away. And when he heard it again that old reading block lifted. That's what she says. But I know her and that elderberry wine. She gave Joe (Ferret's dad) some the other night. So look out. Anything might happen and probably will.

But I'm not going to mess with boyfriends. White veils and babies are boring. Our new teacher – well, she's something else again. When she smiles at you, you want to lay down the world at her feet. She reads a poem every day. We're making a 'Goodbye School' anthology. I shall keep it *for ever*. She knows my mother's poems. But she knows everything. Her name is Mrs Ferndale and I'm going to be a teacher now I've met her. She has brown eyes like sparkling pools (that's not quite right).

I did think of Ferret as a boyfriend but he said don't be barmy and ran off as fast as he could.

* * *

A Day in 1913 by Minty for Mrs Ferndale

That day we dressed up to come in to school. The boys tucked their trousers into long socks. Girls with long hair wore it in ringlets and bows. Some had pinafores. Everybody wore longer clothes than usual and some people wore boots.

Mrs Ferndale had a long black skirt, a white blouse with pretty tucks in it, a large brooch and a black jacket and boots. She didn't wear her lipstick or nail varnish. She looked beautiful but a bit like her own granny.

My mother made me a dress out of brown and white cotton (sprigged, she called it) and a lace trimmed pinafore over it. She found some clothes for Owen, but he didn't want to wear them, though he put his socks over his trousers.

We'd put all the desks in rows the day before and all round the room, children watched us from faded brown photographs. They didn't smile but stared silently at us, those football teams and cricket teams and plays and pantomimes acted long ago. Lists of spellings, tables and a map of the world mostly coloured red hung on the walls as well.

Mrs Ferndale inspected our hands to see if they were clean and we used pens with thin scratchy nibs we had to dip in the inkwells. This was difficult as those nibs were horrible and the ink got on your hands.

Everyone watched the bamboo cane on Mrs Ferndale's desk. She cracked it and we jumped. It frightened me.

Packed sandwiches in brown paper bags were piled on a table at the back of the class. On a big blackboard held by two wooden pegs on the wooden easel was written

TIMETABLE FOR THE DAY

1 The Lord's Prayer
2 Scripture Story
3 Handwriting – copy the Lord's Prayer from the blackboard
4 Dictation: Keats' 'Ode to Autumn'. Verse One
5 Arithmetic: Addition of £, s, d, lb, oz, yd, ft, in
6 Chant tables
7 Class Reader – 'Heroes of the British Empire'

At playtime we played the old games. Some children brought marbles and skipping ropes and Kelly brought a hoop and a stick.

Mrs Ferndale read to us about Captain Scott's travels and did a drawing on the board which we had to copy exactly.

We sang, 'God of Our Fathers', and 'God Save the King'. We had a king then, not a queen.

The Headmaster came in to inspect our work.

I enjoyed the whole day very much. It suited me, but some children did not like it. I don't want another one.

* * *

From Minty's Private Book

Had a 'Walk Back Through Time' exhibition of artefacts and music from 1960 back to 1800 (all items lent by parents, friends, staff, children), 1800 back to the Romans, some items from Museum and children's project work. Kids and public trooped past hundreds of items: mini-dresses, coronation tea-sets, incendiary bombs, wind-up gramophones, a captured First World War German typewriter, Suffragette magazines, Victorian lace, copperplate letters, a commode, old tools etc. At the end they were presented with a certificate: 'This is to certify that *you* walked back in time.'

PS   Mrs Ferndale asked me later if I'd found the day frightening, the silence and the discipline and the cane.

'Not half as bad as an ordinary day with Mrs Flint . . .'

'. . . I didn't hear that!'

'. . . you see it's the teacher, Miss, that makes the difference.'

We said goodbye to Chief Sir. I cried but he smiled as he was presented with – wait for it – a wheelbarrow and a set of gardening tools. Ours, presented by Penelope, was a geranium in a pot.

'Doesn't look much,' I whispered to Ferret.

'Wonder where the money went this time?' he whispered back.

'Shush,' said Beany, looking down his nose. He's getting very bossy these days.

Wonder what he'll be like at our new school? But forget it. I'll worry about *that* later. HOLIDAYS FIRST!

A duck waddled into a library and borrowed some books. The next day the duck waddled in again and got out some more books. On the third day the librarian was very surprised to see the duck come in again, so she followed the duck who led her to a pond.

And there on a waterlily leaf sat a frog croaking, 'Reddit, reddit, reddit.'

Sent by Sharron Harwood

Which is – it's just gotta be –
THE END.

Acknowledgements

Acknowledgements are due to: Janice Cole, Chair, Devon Dyslexia Association; Mary Kibel and the Exwick Reading Workshop; Mrs Janice Davies and Mrs Sally Paddon of St Sidwells School, Exeter, for all their help, information and encouragement (*The Day in 1913* was taken from Mrs Janice Davies's teaching records); Hazel Harvey for extracts from *Discovering Exeter 5*, Sidwell Street; and Jenny Lloyd, Head of English, Vincent Thompson School, Exeter, for extracts from *People Talking*, Volume 7.

The cartoon on page 98 is reproduced by kind permission of *Punch*.

Other books by Gene Kemp

THE TURBULENT TERM OF TYKE TILER

Tyke Tiler is very fond of jokes – that's why there are so many in this story. And Tyke is also fond of Danny Price, who is not too bright and depends a lot on his friend. In fact, medium bright Tyke and medium dim Danny add up to double trouble, especially during their last term at Cricklepit Combined School.

CHARLIE LEWIS PLAYS FOR TIME

For Charlie Lewis and his friends in class 4M, the last term of Cricklepit Combined School *could* have been fun. That is, if the beloved Mr Merchant hadn't broken several bones in the holidays and been replaced by the unbearable Mr Carter (alias Garters). As it is, they've just got to make the best of it – a difficult task for the dynamic Trish Moffat and her lovable but eccentric twin brother, Rocket, who's always getting into trouble; and worse still for quiet, unassuming Charlie whose famous mother just happens to be Mr Carter's favourite concert pianist . . .

GOWIE CORBY PLAYS CHICKEN

Gowie Corby is the terror of Cricklepit Combined School. He's mean, and he wants no help and no friends – apart from Boris Karloff, his pet rat. So when an ancient cellar is uncovered at the school, with ghosts and all, nothing is surely going to prevent him from spending a night there. Especially when he'll be called chicken if he doesn't.

THE CLOCK TOWER GHOST

Addlesbury Tower is haunted by Rich King Cole, a mean old man who fell off it long ago in mysterious circumstances. Its newest terror is Mandy – feared by her family and eventually by the ghost too. In the war they wage to dominate the tower, Mandy and King Cole do frightful and funny things to each other, little guessing how much they really have in common.

JUNIPER

Since her dad left Juniper and her mum have had nothing but problems and now things are just getting worse — there are even threats to put Juniper into care. Then she notices two suspicious men who seem to be following her. Who are they? Why are they interested in her? As Christmas draws nearer Juniper knows something is going to happen . . .

JASON BODGER AND THE PRIORY GHOST

When Jason Bodger, school menace and student teacher's nightmare, visits a priory with Class 4Z, he has a most peculiar and disturbing experience. He sees a strange girl walking towards him high up on a non-existent beam. Mathilda de Chetwynde, born in a castle over 700 years ago, has decided that Jason is just the person she's been waiting for — and there's not a thing Jason can do about it! A hilarious, riotous tale in which the twentieth century meets the Middle Ages!

THE WELL

A secret hideway, dragons in the well, broken vases and hidden Easter eggs: these are just some of the vivid memories which Annie Sutton (alias Gene Kemp) recalls in these perceptive tales of childhood. Living in a Midlands village in the years before the Second World War with her parents her much-loved brother Tom and three grown-up sisters, Annie finds life full of surprises and fears, disappointments and delights.

WAR BOY
Michael Foreman

Barbed wire and barrage balloons, gas masks and Anderson shelters, loud bangs and piercing whines – the sights and sounds of war were all too familiar to a young boy growing up in the 1940s.

Lowestoft, a quiet seaside town in Suffolk, was in the front line during World War II. Bombing raids, fires and trips to the air-raid shelters became almost daily events for young Michael Foreman and his friends.

But gas masks were great for rude noises, gobstoppers were still good to suck and the Hill Green Gang could still try to beat the Ship Road Gang. Father Christmas would tell tales of his days as a cabin boy on the great clippers, the old tramp could spin a good yarn round the camp fire, and nothing could beat Mrs Ruthern's rabbit pie!

OUR KID
Ann Pilling

Frank has high hopes that the money from his paper round will solve all his problems, but the new job plunges him into another world. He meets Tim, with his rich family and his gorgeous sister Cass, and Sister Maggie at the convent (why, he wonders, do nuns read the *TV Times*?) Then there's Foxy, hanging about the streets at all hours.

Frank emerges from this warm and fascinating novel with a new view of his slob of a big brother, his lonely dad, and Foxy, the cat burglar, and discovers 'the amazing things people will do for love'.

THE SPELL SINGER AND OTHER STORIES
ed. Beverley Mathias

The lively, enterprising children in these stories all have some form of disability, and they also have some marvellous adventures. One foils a handbag snatch, another struggles to save the live of a wood-pigeon, one learns to swim with seals in the sea, and one helps solve a bank robbery.

Including writers as varied as Joan Aiken, Vivien Alcock, Allan Baillie, Michael Morpurgo and Geraldine Kaye, this is a hugely enjoyable collection of stories. It is published in association with The National Library for the Handicapped Child.

MAN IN MOTION

Jan Mark

Once Lloyd has started at his new school, he soon finds he's playing cricket with Salman, swimming with Kenneth, cycling with James and playing badminton with Vlad. But American football is Lloyd's greatest enthusiasm. And in time it tests his loyalties, not only to his other sporting activities, but also to the new friends he shares them with.

THE OUTSIDE CHILD

Nina Bawden

Imagine suddenly discovering you have a step-brother and -sister no one has ever told you about! It's the most exciting thing that's ever happened to Jane, and she can't wait to meet them. Perhaps at last she will become part of a 'proper' family, instead of forever being the outside child. So begins a long search for her brother and sister, but when she finally does track them down, Jane finds there are still more surprises in store!

THE FOX OF SKELLAND

Rachel Dixon

Samantha's never liked the old custom of Foxing Day – the fox costume especially gives her the creeps. So when Jason and Rib, children of the new publicans at The Fox and Lady, find the costume and Jason wears it to the fancy-dress disco, she's sure something awful will happen.

Then Sam's old friend Joseph sees the ghost of the Lady and her fox. Has she really come back to exact vengeance on the village? Or has her appearance got something to do with the spate of burglaries in the area?

FLOWER OF JET

Bell Mooney

It's the time of the miners' strike. Tom Farrell's father is branded with the word Tom most dreads; Melanie Wall's father is the strike leader. How can Tom and Melanie's friendship survive the violence and bitterness of both sides? Things are to grow far worse than they ever imagined, for Melanie and Tom discover a treacherous plot that could destroy both their families. And they have to act fast if they're going to stop it.

MIGHTIER THAN THE SWORD

Clare Bevan

Adam had always felt he was somehow special, different from the rest of the family, but could he really be a modern-day King Arthur, the legendary figure they're learning about at school? Inspired by the stories they are hearing in class, Adam and his friends become absorbed in a complex game of knights and good deeds. All they need is a worthy cause for which to fight. So when they discover that the local pond is under threat, Adam's knights are ready to join battle with the developers.

Reality and legend begin to blur in this lively, original story about an imaginative boy who doesn't let a mere wheelchair stand in his way of adventure.

AGAINST THE STORM

Gaye Hicyilmaz

'As Mehmet is drawn into his parents' ill-considered scheme to go and live in Ankara, the directness and the acute observation of Gaye Hicyilmaz carry the reader with him ... Terrible things happen: illness, humiliation, death. But Mehmet is a survivor, and as the book closes, "a sort of justice" has been done, and a satisfying victory achieved. It is a sort of justice too ... that in all the dire traffic of unpublishable manuscripts something as fresh and powerful as this should emerge' – *The Times*